Changing the Channel

Felicity Lerouge

To Justin,
For your unique blend of challenge and support

Changing the Channel

Felicity Lerouge

Cover illustration, book design and setting by;
Neil Coe www.cartadesign.co.uk
Set in Times Roman 9.5 on 15pt

First published in 2009 by;
Ecademy Press
6 Woodland Rise, Penryn, Cornwall UK TR10 8QD
info@ecademy-press.com   www.ecademy-press.com

Printed and Bound by;
Lightning Source in the UK and USA

Printed on acid-free paper from managed forests. This book is
printed on demand, so no copies will be remaindered or pulped.

ISBN-978-1-905823-49-9

Acknowledgements

With gratitude to Tony and Sage Robbins for inspiring ordinary people to live extraordinary lives. Much appreciation goes to my reader panel, Kim Snyder, Sarah Metcalfe, Jan Milikin, Lydia Lambert, Joanna Magiera, Sonia Palacek and Justin Zalewski for your invaluable support and feedback, to Connie Schottky for being my empowering angel and to my exceptionally talented writing coach, Mindy Gibbins-Klein, without whom I would probably have taken the next twenty years to write the book.

Finally, heartfelt thanks go to my dear friend, Chloe Bean, who was also directly responsible for Changing the Channel being written. If she hadn't frightened me into going to the doctor with my ankle injury by saying, "If you don't get that, sorted out, you might never be able to wear pretty shoes again," I would never have discovered I had ruptured my Achilles tendon, which lead to five months off work, during which time I wrote the story's first draft. I'm in your debt, Chloe. I couldn't have worn flat shoes for the rest of my life.

Contents

Chapter 1

Lily looked around the reception and felt a rising sense of horror. Everywhere people were greeting each other like long-lost friends, hugging and kissing with genuine affection. She felt revolted.

A banner rippled gently, illuminated by the torches lining the beach. It announced proudly 'The Ultimate Peer Group welcomes you to the Oneness Experience'.

'The Ultimate Peer Group!' More like the ultimate nightmare! Lily's chest was constricting and she felt close to tears. Turning away from the happy scene, she crouched to retrieve her handbag from under the table where she'd left it only five minutes earlier. Her hands shaking, she fumbled for her room key and made ready to escape from the party.

"Sweetie! You can't possibly leave yet! You've only just arrived." A well-spoken English voice cut across Lily's thoughts and she looked up to see who was speaking to her.

Her eyes took in a statuesque blonde. The woman was dressed simply in a white shift-dress but it was exquisitely cut and complemented her glowing tan and feminine figure. Lily immediately felt small and insignificant. She'd worn her favourite dress this evening, a body-hugging scarlet creation, because it always made her feel fabulous, like a diminutive Angelina Jolie; wearing that dress, she could face anything. Sadly, its effect had been ebbing away since she'd arrived at the reception. The blonde tossed her shoulder-length hair in a gesture that communicated both impatience and amusement.

"Well, come on! You can't stay down there all night."

"But I was just going back to my room, I think the jet-lag is getting to me."

"Nonsense!" The woman took Lily's arm and helped her up. "If you go to bed now you'll never adjust to the time change and we're only here for a week. Besides, I need someone new to play with. I know all this lot already and this evening they're boring me. I'm

Stella by the way – and you're Lily."

"Yes, pleased to meet... how do you know my name?" Stella's commanding presence was making Lily dithery. She found herself being propelled against her will, back across the sand, towards the gathering.

"Sweetie, I make it my business to find out all about the newbies (horrid phrase, don't you think?) I was delighted to find out that there was going to be another Brit to swell our numbers among all these Yanks. It's your first event with UPG, isn't it? It's a bit daunting at first – all those loud voices shrieking at each other – but it's a pretty good bunch and you'll have a fabulous time if you just relax and join in."

Lily thought that Stella's was easily the loudest voice she had heard all evening and certainly the most tactless but she seemed to be the only one to be offended by her insensitive comments. A small group at the edge of the party had opened up to include them as they approached and were laughing at Stella's last remark.

"Stella!" A preppy-looking man in his mid-forties dropped his arm from around the shoulders of the pretty red-headed woman who was cuddled up next to him and enveloped Stella in a bear hug. "We love you, even though all you ever do is bitch about us!"

"Tom, darling! You know I don't mean a word of it." Stella was looking at the couple with great fondness, which had softened her rather impatient features. "Gina! You are the best advert for pregnancy I know." She exchanged a gentle hug with the redhead and stroked her stomach tenderly. "How's number five coming along?"

"Number five is doing great but unfortunately the mother has been a bit hysterical lately."

"Yes," laughed Tom. "I was beginning to think that Gina had an evil twin sister who had appeared out of the dim and distant past, kidnapped her and taken over her life."

"Watch it!" countered his wife, indignantly. "The evil twin can be summoned at any moment, should I need her. You should be more respectful of a pregnant woman's hormones!"

Lily watched the three friends catching up, absorbed in their conversation and thought she might take the opportunity to sneak back to her room. She was just about to start edging away when she felt a hand on her elbow.

"Don't mind them. They're really close but don't get to see each other very often, so sometimes they forget their manners." Lily turned to a third member of the little group they had joined and realised that he was far better-looking than she had appreciated initially in the dim torchlight. Tall, athletic, with brooding dark looks, he conjured up an image of Heathcliffe in *Wuthering Heights*. Lily felt all eloquence desert her, plunging her into an even deeper sense of wretchedness. Thankfully, Stella had overheard the remark and was exchanging playful banter with him.

"Now, Scott, don't cast aspersions on my good name."

"Aspersions? Are they some sort of flower? Would you prefer I threw rose petals?"

"Yes, darling. And you can feed me grapes, too!"

Scott laughed, "That's about as likely as snowfall in the Sahara."

Lily smiled at the exchange and felt herself starting to relax. These were friendly, genuine people and she would soon feel more a part of the group.

"So, how long have you known the others?" she asked Scott.

"Well, Tom and I have known each other since high school. We both met Gina and Stella at college. Not that Stella was a student there, but she may as well have been, the amount of time she spent on campus. Tom fell in love with Gina as soon as he set eyes on her, swept her off her feet within a couple of weeks; they've been together ever since."

"They seem very happy," said Lily and watched Gina tuck herself back under Tom's arm, who dropped a kiss on the top of her head.

"They are. I've never met a couple who are so happy, even after twenty years. They really get each other, you know?" Lily wasn't sure but she thought she detected a trace of wistfulness in Scott's voice. She was about to comment that, no, sadly, she had never had the pleasure of such understanding in a relationship, when an immaculate blonde with artfully-spiked hair sauntered up.

"Hello, my love. Talking about us?" She snaked her arm around Scott's waist and regarded Lily with a basilisk-like stare. "You're a newbie, I haven't seen you before."

"Marcie, this is Lily. It's her first trip with UPG. Stella was introducing us." Scott's attempts at social graces fell on deaf ears. Having stated her claim on him, Marcie had already lost interest in Lily and had turned her attention to Stella.

"Stell, love the Armani! Did you buy it when you were in Europe last week?"

"Oh, hi Marcie." The two women exchanged kisses, Stella having to stoop to reach the petite blonde's cheek. "Yes, I did. It's lovely, isn't it? Though nothing compared to our new friend's delectable Vivienne Westwood." She smiled across at Lily. "You have excellent taste, my dear."

Lily felt a rush of gratitude towards Stella. Her kindness in countering Marcie's snub was thoughtful and showed a sensitivity that Lily wouldn't have expected from her. All the same, the evening was becoming more than she could cope with. That Marcie woman was a bitch. She'd obviously thought that Lily was throwing herself at Scott, which was the last thing on her mind. She'd joined UPG to make some new friends, perhaps network a little and have some fun but she wasn't looking to start a new relationship. The split from her husband the previous year had been painful for them both.

Thankfully, things were amicable again after dealing with the initial hurt and recriminations. Matt had finally agreed that they were going in different directions and that it would be better to finish the relationship sooner rather than later and avoid descending into bitterness and resentment. Lily had promised herself some time on her own to find out what she wanted for her life, without being distracted by having to consider someone else. Not that Marcie would appreciate any of this; she clearly had her pegged as a husband-poacher.

Lily stayed with them for a little while longer before excusing herself, saying she was too tired to stay awake any longer and, despite their protests, made her way back to her room. The solitude was very welcome after the noisy exuberance of the party. She slipped out of her beautiful dress and hung it in the wardrobe, then shrugged on the dressing gown provided by the hotel and went into the bathroom. Pulling her long dark hair back from her face, she started to take off her make-up, reflecting on the strangeness of her behaviour at the reception. It was completely out of character for her to feel insecure with people. She loved socialising and thrived on making new friends, learning about people's lives, hearing about their experiences. As an agony aunt for a teen magazine, she prided herself on her empathy and communication skills but they had both deserted her this evening. Her reflection's green eyes stared steadily back from the mirror but gave nothing away.

"The eyes are the windows of the soul," Lily murmured to herself. "What am I hiding?"

Her image remained mute. Sighing, she switched off the bathroom light, padded across to the bed and climbed in. Tomorrow would put things into better perspective. Once they reached Pele she would feel more relaxed. The brochure she'd been sent proclaimed the resort as being 'A haven of peace and tranquillity in an idyllic island setting' which the photos certainly seemed to confirm. There was something about being near the water that Lily found very calming; she was looking forward to spending some time doing nothing more than gazing into the beautiful azure ocean.

Drifting off to sleep, she dreamt of a little man in a white suit. "Look boss! It's the plane, the plane." Ricardo Montalban regarded his diminutive companion fondly, then fixed Lily with a beatific smile. "Hello, my dear. Welcome to Fantasy Island."

Chapter 2

"Scott! We're going to be late, get up!"

Scott opened one eye, just in time to see Marcie's perfect nakedness disappearing into the bathroom. He glanced at the alarm clock.

"It's only five o'clock. The flight isn't until seven-thirty. Why do we have to get up so early? The airport's only ten minutes away."

Marcie's head appeared around the bathroom door. She paused from cleaning her teeth vigorously and replied, "I want to be there early so that we can get a seat on the first flight; if we don't, we could be hanging about at the airport all day. I want to get to the island in time to explore and take pictures before the seminar starts."

"At least, come back to bed for a little while." Scott curved his slow seductive smile at Marcie, stretching his hand out towards her.

"No time." She disappeared back into the bathroom.

Scott pursed his lips ruefully and, tucking his hands behind his head, lay back on the pillows. There hadn't been a lot of time for anything much lately. He felt as though he was spending his life dashing from one thing to another, propelled along by Marcie's unquenchable energy. When they'd first started dating they'd been hailed by New York society as the new golden couple, the envy of the city's glitterati. They appeared constantly in celebrity magazines as the press followed their careers and shadowed them from one social event to another. Marcie was making a name for herself as a promising young attorney and he, heir to the Pioneer Sportswear dynasty, could do no wrong. It had all seemed such a blast, one gathering of the elite blurred into the next and they were the king and queen of it all. Scott couldn't remember when he had started to feel jaded by the lifestyle that so many people dreamed of but now the thought of going to yet another celebrity party bored him senseless.

None of the excitement had worn off for Marcie. She'd been made a partner in the distinguished law firm of Epstein and Bratch last year, a triumph on two counts as she was the youngest lawyer they'd ever appointed *and* she was female. Her star had continued to rise as she won a number of significant cases, the most notable being her conviction against Michael Tallyard, the soap-opera star, who had murdered his wife in a fit of rage when she announced she was leaving him for her girlfriend. Marcie was right on track for senior partner and nothing had better get in her way.

Scott could recall when all that drive and ambition had been a powerful aphrodisiac but now it just left him feeling tired, which was just as well because Marcie didn't seem to have much time for sex lately. When she did find time in her schedule for love-making, it was performed like a perfectly-executed gymnastic routine. Scott was beginning to suspect that she fitted him in on days that she didn't have time to go jogging in Central Park.

Marcie emerged from the bathroom, immaculately made up and attired in designer casual. Seeing Scott still in bed, she raised one eyebrow in disapproval and huffed resentfully.

"Well, I can see you're not even going to try to make an effort to enjoy this week. I don't know why you agreed to come."

"Chill, Marcie. I am making an effort but it's quarter to six in the morning, for goodness sake!"

"Well, I'm going for breakfast. I've booked a taxi for six-thirty so please make sure you're down in time." She stomped across the room in her Haviaña flip-flops, slamming the door on the way out.

So much for Oneness! Scott considered the theme of the week with wry amusement. There wasn't much evidence of a connection between him and Marcie at the moment; to be honest, he didn't even feel very connected to himself. He didn't understand his lack of satisfaction with his life; he had a great position in the family company, was living with a beautiful, successful woman that he respected and loved, was surrounded by friends, lacked for nothing materially and was as fit and healthy as when he was playing semi- professional baseball at college. He didn't understand what had happened to his vitality and it depressed him. Constantly remonstrating himself for his ungratefulness only made him feel more dejected; he felt that he was slipping into a downward spiral.

Marcie had been impatient when he had tried to talk to her about it.

"It's probably a hormone imbalance. Make an appointment with Dr Hausser and have him run some tests." She'd made him feel like a teenage girl discussing PMS and he hadn't broached the subject again.

They'd spent the Easter break with Tom and Gina at the couple's sprawling homestead, just outside Boston. It had been a great weekend, hiking in the woods with the children tearing about like puppies and Gina keeping everyone supplied with her delicious food. The two men had decided to go fishing very early on the Sunday morning and left for the trout lake as it was just getting light.

The first rays of sunlight were shimmering on the water's surface like a kaleidoscope as they pulled up in Tom's old truck. Scott took in the scene with obvious pleasure.

"You sure live in Paradise," he smiled at his old friend. "Thanks for having us down this weekend."

"That's the first time I've seen you show a spark of life since you got here." Tom's forehead wrinkled with concern. "What's going on, man?"

"I don't know. I look at my life and I've got everything but ... I feel like something's missing ... I know that sounds totally self-indulgent. Don't tell me! I beat myself up over it all the time."

Tom was silent for a moment, gazing out over the lake, before responding.

"You know, I was at the same place as you last year," he began. "My career was exactly as I wanted it, being offered the position of Head of Paediatrics at the hospital was what I'd been working for ever since medical school. Gina and I couldn't have been happier, Archie had just been born and was thriving; life should have been idyllic but instead I kept asking myself whether there was more than this." He laughed. "It was around my fortieth birthday and I thought I was having a mid-life crisis, couldn't find any other explanation for how I was feeling."

"What turned it around for you?" Tom had aroused Scott's curiosity.

"Well, answers can come in surprising packages. Stella had come to stay and was raving about a crowd she'd hooked up with called the Ultimate Peer Group."

"Stella raved?" Scott raised his eyebrows.

"Exactly." Tom nodded. "That's what got our attention. This group apparently organises lectures from the top speakers in every field, from health to finances, people like Deepak Chopra and Suze Orman, and then hosts the seminars in exotic settings all over the world. She said it was some of the most innovative thinking she'd come across since she graduated from Oxford. Outside the lectures, they had free time to just kick back and relax, explore the locations, go sight-seeing, eat the local food, whatever they want. Stella had just come back from her second trip – they meet every third month or so – and couldn't wait to tell us all about it. She said she'd had an amazing time and made some great new friends. She wanted us to join and go to the next meeting."

Scott frowned. "Sounds a bit like a cult."

"That crossed our minds, too," Tom agreed. "But we knew that Stella was much too shrewd to get mixed up in something flaky … and she seemed so happy. She's always had that air of amused boredom about her but now she seemed enthusiastic about life, had lost a few pounds and had taken up her photography again." Tom shrugged. "It made us think and we figured 'what the heck', we could go on one trip and if we didn't like it, we wouldn't go again."

"And?"

"It was the best gift we'd given ourselves for years." The sincerity of Tom's words was unmistakable. "The people were great; they were from diverse walks of life: business people, professionals, artists – all different backgrounds, too. The one thing in common was that everyone wanted to really live life. They were hungry to expand their experience, to improve their relationships, take on the next challenge in their careers, become smarter financially. They were really inspiring." Tom warmed to his theme. "The best part was that they were so willing to share their knowledge and resources. You know, most of the time, when people get a bit of success they feel they need to hoard it for themselves and not tell anyone how they got there? Not this group, they're all about synergy."

"So what's the incentive for all this benevolence?" Scott's tone was still sceptical.

"It makes you feel so good about yourself," Tom smiled. "It's that simple. How many times have you had a goal: to find the girl of your dreams or get that promotion and, when you've attained it, you realise that it didn't give you the feelings you were hoping for. The sense of achievement wears off and often you're left with a nagging sense of emptiness. Tony Robbins, the founder of life-coaching, says that people are only really fulfilled in life if they continue to grow and contribute beyond themselves. Helping other people reach their potential is the inspiration behind the Ultimate Peer Group."

Tom stretched. "I've got carried away with my theme." He turned his attention to the ripples dancing on the lake's surface.

"Those fish look like they're biting and we promised the girls we'd be bringing home lunch. It'll be more like supper if we don't start moving."

"Yeah, and Marcie's pissed off enough with me at the moment," Scott joked as he climbed out of the truck.

Tom gave his friend a pensive look but didn't comment. They'd done enough philosophising for one morning and there were fish to be caught.

That evening Gina had brought up the subject again over dinner and asked if they would be interested in signing up for the next trip. Scott had been prepared for Marcie to discount the idea out of hand but she had been enthusiastic, saying those were exactly the type of people she would want as potential clients. He had smiled quietly at her inherent ability to see a business opportunity in any situation.

Good for Marcie, always so focused, he had thought. If only I had her drive.

Scott came back to the present with a jolt and grabbed the alarm clock: it read 6:55 a.m. He'd only been daydreaming for ten minutes. Still, it was ten minutes well spent. He felt better about the decision to come on the trip after remembering his weekend in Boston. The conversation with Tom that morning had stirred something inside him. He couldn't really put into words what it was, except that he wanted that same sense of ease and self- acceptance that Tom seemed to have found. Yes, it would be nice to feel good about himself. Whistling, Scott swung himself out of bed and sauntered towards the shower.

Chapter 3

Lily sat bolt-upright in bed. She had no idea where she was or what had woken her. She didn't have to ponder the question for long before there was persistent rapping on the bedroom door, accompanied by Stella admonishing her loudly to open up. Of course. She was at the Ultimate Peer Group seminar. Her heart swelled with excitement then contracted with fear, all within a split second, leaving Lily in a state of confusion. The rapping came again.

"I hope there's a fire, or some other emergency, for you to be making all this racket," she barked as she flung open the door. To her chagrin, she found herself face-to-face with both Stella and Scott, both of whom were fully dressed. Lily stood barefoot, wearing a rather skimpy white slip, with her eye-patches shoved back on top of her head. She was well aware that she looked, as well as sounded, slightly demented.

"Sorry, darling," said Stella, cheerfully, "but we thought there might have been an emergency since you didn't turn up for your flight ... and the mood you were in last night, I thought you might have bolted back to the UK."

Lily was deciding if she could rally the necessary dignity to defend herself against the accusation of moodiness, or whether it would require more clothes, when Stella's words sank in.

"Oh my God! Late! I don't believe it!" Her voice rose to a wail. "I'm not packed! Bloody alarm clock!"

"Scott, could you be a sweetheart and phone the airport? Let them know all is well and we'll be with them in about 30 minutes. I'll help Lily pack and we'll meet you downstairs when we're ready." Stella had already started moving about the room, picking up various items of clothing.

"Sure," he smiled consolingly at Lily. "Don't worry, we've all done it. I overslept for Tom's wedding and I was the groom's man; they had to fit in two more hymns before I arrived with the rings.

See you in a little while."

Lily held it together until she heard his steps receding down the corridor then burst into noisy sobs.

"Come and sit down." Stella put her arm around Lily's shoulders and guided her to the bed. "What's brought on the tears?"

"He was nice to me." Lily succumbed to another bout of sobbing.

"Well, Scott's a nice man but that's no reason to be crying," Stella cajoled her gently.

"I'd rather you'd both been angry, that would have been easier to deal with," mumbled Lily, blowing her nose.

"Well, that wouldn't have helped anything, would it?" Stella gave her shoulders a gentle squeeze. "Now, you go and jump in the shower and I'll finish packing." She held up her hand to silence Lily's protests. "No arguments. Ten years of boarding school made me fabulous at packing suitcases. I defy anyone to do a better job … except, perhaps, the butlers at the Burj Al Arab … or Matron. Go on. You'll feel much better after a shower."

Stella was right. As the warm water coursed down her body, Lily felt her distress melt away. She hadn't had a good cry like that for years and it had left her feeling strangely calm. It was astounding how you could bottle up emotion like that without realising it and then, whoosh! One relatively small problem could trigger a *tsunami*. And Stella and Scott had been so kind. She wouldn't have expected that from strangers. Perhaps the next few days would be fun after all. A tentative smile crept across her face and she started to hum. Funny that Scott had come along like that; perhaps Stella thought she'd need him to break the door down. Lily imagined herself being carried from the scene, her inert body cradled in his strong arms, and burst out laughing. Too many romantic novels as an impressionable teenager, she surmised, stepping out of the shower.

Stella was relieved to hear Lily laughing. The poor thing obviously hadn't been used to anyone showing her any kindness for a while. She was glad Lily hadn't escaped on the morning flight to Heathrow. Hopefully, the seminar would give her the opportunity to open up and make some new friends. Maybe it would get to the bottom of whatever it was that was making her so wobbly at the moment.

"That was quick," Scott smiled up from his paper. "Who would have thought, only a few minutes ago you were…?"

"Please, stop!" groaned Lily, interrupting him. "That horrible scenario is going to haunt my dreams as it is. The only thing that could have made it worse was if you'd had a camera."

"Another *You Tube* opportunity lost," Scott shook his head, sadly. "Never mind, I'm sure there'll be plenty more from the group this week. You look very nice, by the way."

Lily smoothed the skirt of her jade-green sundress, shuffling her feet.

"Right, Stell." Realising he had embarrassed Lily, Scott decided to dispel the awkwardness. "I'll go and organise a taxi. Back in a minute."

Stella watched his retreating back affectionately. "Such a gentleman, our Scott. And always so much more relaxed when Marcie's not around."

"Where is Marcie?" Lily asked, wishing the flush in her cheeks would subside.

"Oh, she's very much into social positioning. Wanted to get to the island early and make sure they had the best *bure*. She and Scott have reigned unchallenged as the golden couple in New York for years. Marcie likes to have a contingency plan if she thinks there's a chance of being upstaged. Lawyer, you know."

"Have they been married long?"

"Oh, Lily! They're not married!" Stella chuckled with delight. "The thorn in Marcie's side. It's the only argument she hasn't won for the last decade."

"So you don't like her much?" Lily was curious.

"It's not that I don't like her – she's not a bad sort when you know her better – but I find the constant networking exhausting. And unnecessary. Scott's family is one of the richest in the States. There's no need to keep trying to prove they're more important than anyone else."

"Maybe if he married her, she wouldn't feel the need to prove anything," mused Lily.

"Quite possibly," Stella agreed. "Initially, that was all Scott wanted but she was totally focused on her career. The worm has turned over the last couple of years but, for some reason, Scott doesn't seem very keen on the idea now. Marcie's sure she'll win him round but I'm not so sure…"

"Have you known them long?" asked Lily.

"Ages," Stella nodded. "I was at high school with Gina then I was whisked off to university in England but I used to slope off when I got bored, jump on a plane and spend a few days on campus with Gina, Tom and Scott, camping out in Gina's room. Trust fund," she replied to Lily's inquisitive look. "My father, Mummy's third husband, was Lord Ratcliffe. Didn't see much of him after he left – I was five – but he had oodles of money and very generous with it, too. Not a bad old codger," she reminisced, "but he never should have married my mother. Biggest gold-digger on the East coast."

"Stella!" gasped Lily.

"What?" she was unrepentant. "I'm only repeating what she told me. Scarlet O'Hara was her role-model, she always said. Here's our taxi. Lovely!" Stella strode off on long golden legs.

"It's a bit small, isn't it?" Lily was looking dubiously at the

Cessna.

"It'll be fine for the three of us." Scott surveyed the small aircraft confidently. "Are you girls ready to have your luggage loaded?"

They both nodded and Scott called over a small, bright-eyed local. "Load up the bags, would you, Sunia, I'm just going to do the walk-round."

"What's he doing?" asked Lily.

"He's just doing the routine checks before take-off," Stella explained.

"Well, surely that's the pilot's job," said Lily, bemused.

Her companion gave an exasperated sigh. "He is the pilot. All the flights UPG had organised have already left. This was the only way we could get to Pele today, so Scott chartered the Cessna."

"Don't look so despairing," laughed Stella, seeing Lily's stricken expression. "Scott loves to fly and was glad to have the excuse to stay behind and offer his expertise when you didn't arrive this morning. You made his day."

"I must offer to share the cost," said Lily, anxiously.

"Don't you dare!" Stella was adamant. "Scott's 'old school' and would be insulted. Besides," she said, watching him make the last external checks, "he's obviously feeling like a bit of a hero, being able to rescue a damsel in distress. Don't spoil it for him; he gets little enough chance to be Marcie's knight in shining armour."

"You make him sound as though he's Marcie's lap-dog."

Stella shook her head, "It's not that. It's just that he's lost some of his spark over the last couple of years. Marcie has a carefully-planned schedule for everything, which doesn't allow for a lot of spontaneity. Last New Year's Eve we ended up at the same party, an utterly dull affair with the same old faces. Scott was looking rather glum but I thought it was the result of having to endure so much boring conversation. Eventually, I got him to tell me what was causing such a long face. He said he had planned a surprise trip to Venice for Marcie for New Year, but when he presented her with the ticket that morning she had refused to go, saying he hadn't given her enough notice to plan her packing."

"You mean they didn't go?" Lily was incredulous.

"Yes. The whole trip went to waste." Stella grinned. "I wished I'd known earlier; I would have insisted that he took me instead."

"Poor Scott."

"Yes, indeed," agreed Stella. "It's hard enough to find a man who's romantic and generous without throwing it back in his face. One or two incidents like that and it's no surprise he's lost some of his spark."

"Venice…" Lily's lips released a sensuous hiss as she lingered over the last syllable.

"I know." Stella was in complete empathy with her new friend. "Fabulous food, architecture and clothes, plus gorgeous men eager to flirt with you. What was the silly woman thinking of?"

"I have no idea," said Lily, her eyes on Scott.

"I've never seen so many different shades of blue!" exclaimed Lily, turning from the window to talk to Stella. "It's so beautiful."

"You wait until we get closer to Pele, the island is magical," Scott called back through the open cockpit door.

"How long now?" Lily's eyes were wide with excitement.

"We'll start the descent in a few minutes," replied Scott. "You should come and sit up here for the best view."

"Go ahead," Stella smiled at Lily's hopeful expression. "I've sat up there dozens of times."

"Thank you!" Lily darted through the door and scrambled into the co-pilot's seat.

"Do you know how to fasten the safety harness?" asked Scott. "It can sometimes get a bit bumpy on the final approach."

Lily clicked the buckles into place. "I'm all in; you can loop the loop now if you want to," she said cheerfully.

"I'd be happy to, but this isn't my plane."

"Can you really do that?" she asked, her eyes even wider.

"No, no!" laughed Scott, enjoying her exuberant mood. "But I can juggle peas."

Lily pulled a face. "That's not nearly so impressive."

"Really? They are *petits pois*."

They both began to snicker at the absurdity of the conversation.

"What's going on up here?" Stella leaned into the cockpit. "Am I missing a good joke? Oh, look, Lily! There's Pele, down there, on the left."

Lily was enchanted with her first glimpse of the island. A ring of bright azure encircled its golden beaches which, in turn, bordered lush tropical forest. The main *bure* at the resort could be spied through the trees, at the edge of a clearing, with various smaller structures dotted about. The place had an air that was both welcoming and mysterious. Lily felt a *frisson* of excitement run through her. She beamed at her two companions. "It's just like that 70's show *Fantasy Island*."

"Isn't it?" Scott nodded enthusiastically. "The first time I came here, I expected Mr Roarke and Tattoo to walk out of the main *bure*."

"Ricardo Montalban!" squealed Lily in delight. "I dreamt of that exact scene last night!"

"What! You dreamt of that horrid, wrinkly old man!" Stella was appalled.

"Not that kind of fantasy," said Lily in mock disapproval. "*Fantasy Island* was where wealthy guests paid to have their dreams come true."

"Yes," Scott joined in, "but often they didn't turn out as they had expected."

"No, but they always got the lesson they needed," added Lily. She looked bemused. "Don't you remember the show, Stella?"

"No I don't," she retorted, "and from your brief summary, I can't think that I've missed very much."

"Not heard of *Fantasy Island*!" Scott was disbelieving. "Man, I loved that show as a kid. I even tried to persuade my mom to buy me the white trouser suit."

"Thankfully, your mother is a very sensible woman would have more sense than to have let you shame the family like that," Stella teased. "Please concentrate on landing now, Scott. I'm starting to feel the need for some adult conversation."

"Who'd have thought I'd be coming to Fantasy Island?" Lily murmured to herself, tracing the coastline with her finger. "I'm going to believe that some of my dreams will come true while I'm here."

Chapter 4

The Cessna taxied along the grass landing-strip and pulled up in front of a battered tin construction that served as the airport building. Descending from the small aircraft, Lily saw that Marcie was waiting for them.

"Uh, oh!" muttered Stella from the side of her mouth. "The not-so-welcoming committee. Hello, Marcie darling. How was your morning? Have you been up to the waterfall?"

Marcie, whose face resembled a smacked bottom, ignored Stella's cheery greeting and accosted Scott. "I waited all morning so that we could go and see the waterfall together. Then I find out you've stayed to perform a rescue mission because Somebody couldn't set her alarm clock. Not even a phone call! I wanted our first day here to be special." Marcie's voice trembled as she struggled to keep her anger in check.

"I tried your cell, Honey, but the network said the number was ..."

"Please, Scott," Marcie raised her hand, cutting him off, "I don't want to talk about it in public." She glared at Scott's passengers. "Can we go now?"

"See you later, guys." Scott followed Marcie to her waiting car and they sped off in a cloud of dust.

"Nice of her to enquire how we would get to the resort," observed Stella. "Still, the Oneness guides did say all kinds of unresolved issues come to the surface at an event like this. Ah, look! Here's my dear old friend, Nelson."

"Hello, Miss Stella." An elderly-looking islander had stepped forward out of the shade. "How are you today?"

"Always so solicitous, Nelson. I'm very well, thank you. How are your children and grandchildren – eight, now, isn't it?"

"Nine," replied Nelson with a shy smile, showing his passengers to a waiting jeep. "The last one was born in the Spring. A girl. Happy and healthy, like the rest."

"I'm so pleased to hear it. And how is Noah? Was he accepted by Brunel?"

"Yes, Miss, and he got a scholarship, too."

Stella's pleasure at his news was clearly genuine. Lily tuned in and out of their conversation as they drove along dirt roads at the edge of the glittering ocean. On the other side of the track, exotic trees stood like sentinels, bearing glorious, vibrantly-coloured flowers. The wind tousled her hair and she felt more light-hearted than she had done since her divorce. From time to time, they drove past a cluster of dwellings, or passed some of the villagers on the road. Everyone greeted them with the same wide smile and a cheerful wave, "Welcome, welcome."

"I never imagined it would be so beautiful here," Lily finally broke her silence, "and so tranquil."

"It is a magical place." Stella spoke fondly. "I've been coming here all my life but it never loses its charm for me."

"You're very lucky," said Lily wistfully.

"Yes, I am," agreed Stella. "It was my father's resort. When he died, he left it to me in his Will. It's always been a wonderful place to share with friends. Tom, Gina and I used to come here all the time when we were in our twenties. And Scott, too, with whichever girl he had in tow at the time. When UPG announced that they were proposing a seminar on Oneness I offered them the resort. Thought it would be the perfect location."

"What do you know about Oneness?" asked Lily. "The information they sent us was a bit vague, something along the lines of a spiritual journey that would bring us into a sense of ease with ourselves and those around us. To be honest, it sounded a bit flaky but because UPG has such a good reputation, I decided to take a chance and come along."

"You won't regret it." Stella reassured her. "I met the guides a couple of months ago when they came to see if the resort would be suitable. They are wonderful people."

"You mentioned them at the airport. Who are they?"

"They teach the philosophy of Oneness and take us through a process called *deeksha* or, more commonly, the blessing; it's a kind of energetic re-balancing," Stella explained. "It helps us to realise we are all connected to one another and that our actions affect each other at a profound level; it is the beginning of a sense of Oneness." Seeing the dubious look on Lily's face, Stella laughed. "I know it's a hard concept to grasp but it will be easier once you've experienced it." She thought for a moment. "You know the sense of well-being that you get after you've been on a long run, or done a yoga class? Everything seems to fall away and you're just experiencing the flow of life through your body. Everything else quietens down and you feel as though you could keep going forever. It feels something like that."

"I think I know what you mean," Lily said, thoughtfully. "I feel like that when I dance. I lose track of time and everything just feels right. Is that it?"

"It's very much like that. Anything experienced fully is joy."

The journey continued in silence, both women lost in their own thoughts. Lily was intrigued by what she had just heard. She loved to dance, it made her feel alive and vibrant. It was the vehicle she used when she felt down, to chase away feelings of being sad and alone, to help her forget her problems. Torn between feelings of curiosity and scepticism, she decided she would just go with the flow and see what happened.

They drove through the resort's entrance, flanked by imposing wrought-iron gates. Nelson turned down a narrow grass track and pulled up in front of a pretty wooden structure with a thatched roof.

"Thank you, Nelson," said Stella, accepting his hand as she

stepped down from the jeep. "Jump down, Lily. We're sharing this *bure* for the next few days."

"Really?" beamed Lily, hopping on to the well-kept lawn. "My information pack said I was sharing with someone called Daphne."

"You were," Stella winked, "but I decided to nab you for myself. Daphne can be a bit of a challenge and I thought you'd prefer a more tranquil experience this week. Plus she snores. I shared with her on my first UPG trip and woke up in the middle of the night thinking I'd wandered into a field of cows."

"Well, that's very kind of you," said Lily, gratefully.

"Isn't it? You owe me," Stella retorted, with a grin. "For starters, I get the pick of the bedrooms." She climbed the steps to the front door and fitted a key into the lock. "Come on, I'll show you around."

Marcie was clattering around in the *bure*'s kitchen, making coffee. She still maintained a tight-lipped silence, despite Scott's attempts to coax her out of it.

"Come on, Honey! We're here in paradise. Let's enjoy it," he pleaded.

Marcie slammed the cafetière down on a tray in exasperation.

"I was totally ready to enjoy being here until you abandoned me to play Boy Scout."

"Come on, Marcie, not that again." Scott raised his eyes to implore the heavens. "We went over all that on the drive from the airport. You know nobody else had a pilot's licence."

"You should have let her get the regular flight tomorrow," she snapped. "It's no-one else's fault that she can't set her alarm clock."

"It wasn't that. The hotel didn't give her a wake-up call."

"Don't you dare side with her against me!"

"Look, nobody's taking sides. It isn't a conspiracy." Scott was becoming increasingly annoyed at her childish behaviour.

"I wanted the *bure* with the jacuzzi!" Coffee sloshed over the sides of the cups as Marcie's hand shook with anger. "Because you were late they gave it to that dowdy couple from Minnesota."

"You spoiled brat!" Scott narrowed his eyes and looked at her coldly. "That's all this is about, isn't? Social positioning! I thought you were upset because you were jealous but this is all about status."

"Jealous?" Marcie's rage was replaced by disdain. "Why would I be jealous? You were only with Stella and that little mouse. No competition to worry me there," she added contemptuously.

Scott stared at her in disbelief. "You're unbelievable. I'm going for a walk. I need some fresh air to clear my head from all this bullshit!"

"Don't you dare be late!" Marcie screamed after him. "You've shown me up quite enough for one day."

Lily woke from her nap, to the sound of waves lapping against the shoreline. Leaning up on one elbow, she surveyed her view with a languid yawn. It was picture-postcard perfect: palm trees rose out of the golden sand, inviting beach chairs enticed you to linger at the water's edge and the scent of exotic flowers wafted in through the open window. Lily could have gazed at the panorama for days. Stirring herself from her reverie, she glanced at her watch: 3:05 p.m. The first session wasn't until five o'clock. She might just have enough time to do some exploring. Slipping on her shorts and T-shirt, she wandered out on to the porch.

"Hello, Sleepy Head. Feeling better for a rest?" Stella was swinging gently back and forth on the porch swing, her book on her lap.

Lily stretched like a contented cat. "I feel wonderful. Completely refreshed. You didn't sleep, then?"

"No. I've just been enjoying soaking up all the familiar sights and smells," she smiled. "I feel refreshed just being here."

"It's a quarter past three." Lily checked her watch. "I thought I might go and do some exploring before the meeting. Do you want to come?"

"I'll stay here, if you don't mind. I'd like to finish my book. You should definitely have a look around, though. Go up to the waterfall. Do you see that track, running up the hill?" Lily shaded her eyes to see where Stella was pointing. "That's the path that will take you there. It's well worth the walk. It should take you about twenty minutes."

"Great! I'll see you later." Lily set off, leaving her friend to enjoy the serenity of the porch.

Stella was right; the climb had been well worth the effort. It had been hotter than Lily had expected trudging up the hill but, once she reached the brow, the path curved down again, entering a thicket of trees. Reaching their shade, she continued along the track for a few more minutes, enjoying the sensation of being protected from the tropical sun by the leafy canopy. She could hear cascading water and followed its sound until she was standing at the edge of a large pool. Large outcrops of stone surrounded the water, lush with the verdant foliage springing up in every shade of green. The waterfall tumbled gracefully from the far side of the expanse of water, reminding Lily of the fairy tale character Rapunzel, as she let down her hair from the ivory tower.

It was a glorious oasis and it was all hers. Lily felt she had been given a rare gift. Watching an emerald dragonfly skim over the water, she had an idea. Glancing around to check she was alone, she sat down at the edge of the pool and removed her tennis shoes and socks. She had just begun to unbutton her shorts when a disembodied voice floated down from the dense canopy above her head.

"Lily, as it appears you're going to take off your clothes, I feel honour-bound to alert you to my presence."

Lily screamed, tried to stand up with her shorts around her knees and fell sideways into the crystal-clear water.

"Oh my God!" Scott swung himself down from the branch he'd been sitting on and dropped on to the mossy ground. "Are you all right?"

"Don't come near me, you pervert!" She ignored his outstretched hand and kicked out towards the middle of the pool. "Stalker!"

Scott tried very hard to hold back his laughter but it erupted. Lily's face was so comically indignant that he couldn't help himself. Unfortunately, it only served to make her even more furious.

"How dare you make the situation worse by laughing at me!"

"I'm truly sorry," Scott managed to subdue his laughter but couldn't conceal his evident amusement. "Though, in my defence, I have to point out that I was here first so I couldn't have been stalking you, and if I really was a pervert I would have kept quiet and let you carry on stripping."

"I was NOT stripping!" Lily spluttered in a poor attempt to shout and tread water simultaneously. "I wanted to go for a swim!"

"And you have," he grinned. "How is the water, by the way?"

"Aarrrr!" she fumed and swam off towards the waterfall, clearly not willing to be appeased.

"Not going to tell me? Well, I'll just have to find out for myself." Stripping off his T-shirt, Scott dived into the water.

His strong crawl soon caught up with her prim breast-stroke and he paddled alongside her. "Please, Lily, don't be so cross. It really was very funny." She continued to look straight ahead, her nose haughtily in the air, but her mouth had started to twitch with the beginnings of a smile.

"I knew you'd see the funny side!" Scott was triumphant.

Lily gave up trying to regain her dignity. "It was certainly the most pompous speech a stalker ever gave, 'I feel honour-bound to alert you to my presence ...'"

"OK, OK! I was embarrassed! I was just about to say hello when you started to take your clothes off."

The look Lily gave him was full of recrimination. "Don't talk to me about embarrassment! I've never been so mortified in my life!"

"It will be much worse when I tell everyone else later!" he laughed, darting out of Lily's way as she lunged at him. "I'm kidding! Come on! Swim for the other side. There's a cave behind the waterfall I want to show you."

He pulled himself out of the water first, then, grasping Lily's hand, helped her on to the bank. "Seriously, I wouldn't tell anyone." Scott's expression was solemn. She narrowed her eyes at him in an attempt to look fierce. "I should hope not, you'd have hell to pay."

"Now I'm very afraid," he smiled. "We'll say no more about it."

The cavern behind the waterfall was like a fairy grotto. Miniature ferns hung from crevices in the dome overhead, their delicate leaves adorned with droplets of water that made them shimmer like precious jewels. Light filtered into the space through the curtain of the waterfall, refracting the sunshine in a million rainbow fragments. Lily stooped to gaze into one of the little rock pools. "It's like a tiny world." Her voice was full of wonder when she spoke next. "This is an extraordinary place. Thank you for sharing it with me."

"You're welcome," Scott said happily. "I love it when people see the place for the first time; it reminds me of how special it is."

A smooth ledge of stone jutted out from the cave wall. Lily checked it wasn't too damp, then perched her bottom on it.

"So what were you doing in that tree, anyway?"

His jaw tensed slightly. "Marcie and I had a fight."

"Over this morning?"

"Yes," he nodded. "I thought she was jealous because I was with you and Stella but she was just pissed off because she'd missed out on the *bure* she wanted." He grinned ruefully. "Not great for my ego."

Lily winced. "I'm sorry I got you into trouble."

"Don't be." He was pragmatic. "We've got some stuff we need to work out, that's all. Hopefully this week will help us do that."

Looking up at him, Lily knew that the relaxed, confident, playful man she had seen earlier was the real Scott. She hoped the next few days would help him resolve his issues with Marcie. As her thoughts drifted towards the session that evening, it dawned on her that they had lost track of time. She looked at her watch in panic.

"What's the time? My watch has stopped!"

Realising that they were going to be late, Scott swore under his breath. "Shit! We'll have to get a move on or we'll miss the start of this evening's meeting."

They left the magical cavern and, grabbing their shoes and clothes, hastily began the descent to the bures, Lily having to scurry to keep up with Scott's long strides. Suddenly she burst into giggles.

"What's so funny?" Scott asked, in surprise.

"It's just that so far on this trip I've spent most of the time feeling like a naughty little girl!"

He looked amused. "And were you?"

"According to my mother. I thought my name was Stop-It-Lily until I was about five years old." She shrugged, nonchalantly. "She's never been the easiest woman to please."

Despite her blasé attitude, she was clearly covering up her

feelings. Scott's own parents had always been so supportive; it had come as a shock to him, growing up, that other homes weren't as happy as his. Families could hurt each other so much; it was a great shame.

Aware that a slightly gloomy atmosphere had descended, Lily challenged Scott to a contest.

"Race you to those palm trees!" She shouted and sped off. Scott, of course, caught up with her in seconds.

"This is nuts! I'm practically having to walk here. Maybe I should be running backwards?"

Ignoring him, she focused all her effort into increasing her pace; finding a final burst of energy, she sprinted to the trees, beating Scott by a hair's breadth.

"You let me win," she panted, resting her hands on her knees to ease her pounding chest.

"Of course I did," he agreed. "I'm a gentleman. But that wasn't a bad effort – you should be called Tiger Lily."

She laughed. "That's what my dad used to call me. Tell you what, if we jog the last bit we might have time for a quick wash before the meeting."

"Tell you what!" Scott repeated, delighted with the phrase. "I love the way you Brits speak. It's so quaint!"

"Don't you dare get me started on that subject," she glowered, jogging alongside him at a more sedate pace. "Next thing you'll be telling me that it's OK to have an accent. As I'm an English woman speaking English, it's clearly you Americans that have the accent."

"It is, indeed, a wonderful accent," teased Scott, "but it's a shame you don't spell properly."

Realising she didn't have a suitably witty retort, Lily was glad that they had reached her bure. "This is mine," she said. "See you at the meeting."

"Bye!" Scott peeled off, with a wave to Stella who was waiting on the porch. Lily's room-mate said nothing but raised her eyebrow enquiringly.

"It's a long story; I'll tell you later. Have I got time for a wash?"

Stella looked at her watch. "If you're quick; it's quarter to five. You must fill me in on all the gossip," she said, noting her friend's bedraggled appearance as she darted past. "I feel some scandal has taken place this afternoon," she called after Lily. "How delightful!"

Chapter 5

"Do calm down," Lily hissed at her friend as Stella burst into yet another peal of laughter. She paused outside the door of the main *bure*. "Show a little decorum."

"I'm sorry!" Stella dissolved into mirth once more. "It's just the thought of you, so prim, with your shorts around your ankles! Hee hee!" Leaning against the wall, Stella tried to regain her composure.

"What do you mean, 'prim'?" Lily was indignant.

"You must admit, my dear, you are a little uptight."

"Evening, ladies." It was the couple from Minnesota who had robbed Marcie of her coveted jacuzzi. Their timely arrival diverted Lily from her rising sense of pique.

"Are you going in?" The husband smiled.

"Hello, John. Hello, Brenda," said Stella, recovering herself. "Yes, of course. Have you met Lily?"

Lily nodded hello and they made to enter the *bure*. Opening the door, they stole in quietly, careful not to disturb the mood of quiet expectation that pervaded the room. Stella gestured to a couple of spare seats on the right-hand side and they made their way over to them.

"Mmm, jasmine," she whispered, breathing in the delicate aroma, "and candles. Very atmospheric." She settled comfortably on her seat and closed her eyes, soaking up the ambiance.

The session started. Lily took the opportunity to observe the rest of the group that had gathered for the meeting. Some were talking quietly among themselves and some, like Stella, were letting themselves drift away, lulled by the gentle background music and the scent of jasmine that wafted through the open windows. Scott was sitting on the right-hand side of the room with Tom and Gina. Where was Marcie? Oh, there she was, sitting on the cushions in the front row, in the lotus position, her eyes closed in an attitude of meditation. Despite her pose, there was nothing calm about her

posture. Her whole body screamed with tension. Lily felt a wave
of sympathy for her; it must be terrible to never be able to relax, to
always be thinking about being Number One. Not for the first time,
Lily thanked her father for reminding her of the importance of the
balance between work and play.

"Life is short and sweet, my dear. Nobody on his death bed ever
said he regretted not spending more time at the office." The words
echoed in her mind, conjuring a picture of her father, sitting at that
same desk, books sprawled in front of him and his fingers stained
peacock-blue from his favourite fountain pen.

His words had proved truer than he could have predicted. When
Lily was twenty-four, she lost him to a brain embolism and felt
as though her heart had been torn out. He had died instantly, in
that same chair. The doctor assured them that it would have been
instantaneous and painless. It was something to be thankful for in
the face of the grief they felt with his passing. Lily's mother, who
had done nothing but grumble about him when he was alive, now
found she had nothing to live for and entered deep, bitter depression.
She embraced the role of dejected widow and rounded upon anyone
who tried to alleviate her misery. Lily had long since given up;
never having been her mother's favourite, she now seemed to have
become her anathema. Nothing she could do was right. Her brother,
Paul, could do no wrong, despite the fact that he rarely phoned and
visited even less frequently. Lily tried hard not to resent him; after
all, he had hated being put on a pedestal. He constantly pointed out
all that Lily tried to do for their mother, admonishing the widow for
throwing it back in Lily's face. But to no avail; she was determined
to see her daughter as the black sheep of the family. She had never
got over the fact that Lily had been her father's favourite.

Lily felt the constriction in her chest and realised she'd started
down the old familiar path to her secret insecurities. No, she
wouldn't let herself be overwhelmed by them, not here, among

strangers. She shook her head as if to physically chase the thoughts away and stuck out her chin defiantly. Her father hadn't called her Tiger Lily for nothing; she had fought off her demons for most of her life and she wouldn't let them get the better of her now.

Stella opened her eyes and glanced at Lily. "Is everything all right? You look as though you'd like to hit someone."

"I'm fine, really," Lily waved away Stella's concerns. "Just some old memories. Nothing to worry about."

"Are you sure?" Stella was unconvinced. "Oh, look! There's Raksith."

Glad of the distraction, Lily followed Stella's gaze to see that a handsome Indian man, dressed in a white *shawani* and trousers had appeared at the front of the stage. Slightly behind him were six other similarly-dressed men of the same race.

"Welcome." Raksith's lilting tones brought a hush to the room. Everyone turned towards the stage, curious to hear what this man had to say. "We are the guides from the Oneness University and are very happy to have you here with us this week, as we share our message with you." He smiled. "To help us to get to know you better, we thought it would be easier if we divided you into smaller groups for this evening. The guides will call the names of those in their groups. When you hear your name, please accompany them." He bowed slightly and stepped back.

One of his companions took centre stage. He was taller and wore gold-rimmed spectacles.

"Good evening. My name is Rajesh." His solemn expression was interrupted by a beaming smile. "This is my group: Daphne, Rod, Scott, Marcie, Stella, Tom, Gina, John, Brenda and Lily. Please accompany me to the lounge at the reception. Thank you."

Lily joined the end of the small train that was following the guide, glad to be in the same group as Stella. She suddenly felt a little insecure. They had only spent a matter of minutes in the company of these men but she already had the feeling they had a sense of intuition and wisdom that was uncommon in this modern world. Lily felt that they would see through the veneer she wore in public and she wasn't sure she liked that thought.

Reaching the open lounge next to the resort's reception, Stella, threw herself down on to a sumptuous couch, patting the place next to her in an invitation to Lily. She was just about to join her new friend when a white-haired man with a crabby expression beat her to her seat.

"My old bones are more in need of this seat than your young ones," he muttered gruffly at Lily.

"Please, feel free. I'm happy to sit on the floor," she replied politely, thinking inwardly 'selfish old curmudgeon!' There was a spare bean-bag next to Scott and Marcie but Lily was slightly worried that she might melt under Marcie's fiery gaze if she sat too close to her. Obviously the young woman was still blaming Lily for her current relationship problems and if she knew she'd been with Scott at the waterfall, it was no surprise. Lily sighed inwardly. There would be no point trying to placate her; she was obviously looking for a scapegoat. Hopefully, once the teaching sessions began in earnest, things would be resolved for the couple.

When everyone was finally settled, the guide spoke from the armchair he was occupying, his inflection melodious and soothing.

"I understand that not everyone here knows each other and, as I do not know any of you, perhaps it would be useful to introduce ourselves and say a little about our lives." He inclined his head towards Stella. "Please, would you be kind enough to start?"

"Hi, everyone! I think you all know me. Stella. Forty-five and fabulous! Photographer. Merrily widowed with two delicious boys: Charlie, 14 and Brett, 12."

"Thank you, Stella." Rajesh turned his gaze next to the white-haired man who had beaten Lily to the couch.

"Rod Stein," he growled. "From Texas. I'm in casinos. Divorced twice. No children. Only reason I'm here is to catch up with the friends I've met through UPG. Don't have much time for this Oneness nonsense."

"Thank you, Rod," said the guide without any trace of irony. Neither did he appear to have heard the intake of breath that rippled around the room at the Texan's rudeness. "Please continue," he said, looking at Lily kindly.

"Oh, I'm Lily Butler. English," she said unnecessarily, a little nervous to have the attention of the whole room. "I've just entered my fabulous forties, too. I'm … divorced, an agony aunt for a teenage magazine in the UK and I'm just in the process of writing my first novel." Lily was glad when the guide moved on to the next person. She felt as though she was a candidate at a speed-dating evening. It had been her misfortune to attend one such event and she had been horrified at how quickly people could assess and dismiss you – or decide, as one creepy man had done, that you probably didn't wear any underwear. Returning to the present, she gave her attention to the man on her left, who was introducing himself.

"Hi, I'm John and this is my wife, Brenda. We're from Minnesota. Been married twenty-six years next month," he said proudly, putting his arm around his wife's shoulders. "Two girls and a boy, all grown up now. We're in real estate."

People in the room looked enquiringly at Brenda but she just smiled back. Surely she's not going to let her husband say everything for her, thought Lily but, evidently, she was.

Marcie clearly didn't think Brenda was worth wasting any more time on and interjected.

"Marcie Brauer, attorney. Thirty-five. Youngest female lawyer to ever make partner at Epstein and Bratch, New York. I'm with Scott, of course," she placed a proprietary hand on his knee. Her 'trophy' spoke.

"Hi, everyone, I'm Scott. I'm forty. I work in the family business, which is sportswear and equipment. And I'm very glad to be here with you all this week." He smiled warmly.

"Thank you, Scott." Rajesh turned to the next member of the group, a grey-haired woman in her fifties who had been nodding enthusiastically at every comment. "Please." He opened his hand, inviting her to speak.

The woman rose to her feet in a manner that vaguely reminded Lily of the Reverend Peterson's wife at church meetings, back at home. Her hands clasped at her chest, she addressed the room with slightly brittle enthusiasm.

"Hello everyone, I'm Daphne Carter. I've met many of you already, of course, and it's so good to be among our little group once again. For those of you who don't know, I'm a personal development executive. I am well-qualified, having graduated from a number of schools of therapy, as well as having trained with Guru Raman. Also, I have psychic powers. If any of you has any concerns over the next few days, don't hesitate to contact me, day or night. I shall be very glad to offer my services."

"Steady on, Daphne," quipped Stella. "You'll be doing the guides out of a job." Daphne continued, undeterred. "I wouldn't dream of being so presumptuous, but we all have our skill-sets and, when I'm holding my seminars, I encourage the participants to share their resources," she beamed. "After all, many hands make light work!"

Lily couldn't think of anyone she would be less likely to go to with her problems. She caught Stella's eye who was revelling in Daphne's inappropriate behaviour and mouthed a heartfelt 'thank you.' To think she could have been sharing a room with that impossible woman!

Daphne was drawing breath to continue but Rajesh cut in elegantly, silencing her monologue.

"Thank you, Daphne. I'm sure we are all most grateful for your generous offer. May we now hear from the last of our number?" He graciously inclined his head towards Tom and Gina.

"Hi, guys! I'm Tom."

"And I'm Gina."

"We've been married for fifteen years and, like the old song says, '*It don't seem a day too long*'…" crooned Tom.

"We have four children. Two boys, two girls and another one on the way," continued Gina, stroking her stomach.

"Catholic family!" joked Tom, smiling at his wife.

"No, it's just that I love to bake and I've never worked out how to gauge the quantities for less than eight people!" she laughed. "Thankfully, I've found an outlet for my passion in my tea-rooms. If you're ever in South Boston, drop by for a chat and a pot of tea."

"Gina makes the best carrot cake on the East coast," added Tom. "Thankfully, she takes pity on us over-worked doctors and regularly brings us a batch for the paediatric department's staff room."

The couple looked fondly at one another, momentarily oblivious of anyone else in the room.

"And now I shall tell you a little about myself," said the guide, straightening his white tunic. "My name is Rajesh and I have been at the Oneness University in India for fifteen years. With Ananda Giri-ji and my fellow guides, we share the message that was given to us by the founder of the movement, Sri Amma Bhagavan. The message gives us hope for this world; it comes to us as an act of grace through the blessing, a phenomenon which causes an energetic re-balancing in the brain and ends our feeling of separation from each other." He smiled at the group, his perfect white teeth contrasting vividly with his dark skin. A number of expressions were reflected in the faces of his new students: some looked curious, others looked wary and Rod looked utterly bored.

The Texan yawned loudly, with no attempt to hide his disinterest. Lily couldn't believe that anyone could be so rude and began to blush in embarrassment, out of sympathy for the guide. Once again, Rajesh appeared totally unconcerned. He had certainly heard the yawn; it was so loud he had broken off his discourse until Rod had finished, but he continued speaking without any sign of irritation. Lily wondered how someone could be so gracious in the face of such ignorance.

"During the next few days you will be experiencing the blessing and we will be sharing our teachings with you."

"So, how do we receive this blessing?" ask Scott leaning forward in his seat, his curiosity getting the better of him.

"The guides will give you the blessing in our small groups and then, tomorrow evening, you will receive the blessing from the Oneness Beings who have accompanied us to Pele," he continued. "We will place our hands on your heads for a brief period of time, during which you will receive the transfer of energy that will begin to re-balance your biochemistry."

"Right," Scott looked a little bemused, "and how will that change my biochemistry?"

"It's just like Reiki healing," Daphne interjected before the guide could reply. "We are all made up of the same energy, so that energy can flow from one person to another, given the right training. I'm a Reiki healer myself," she added immodestly.

"Thank you, Daphne," said Rajesh regaining control of the conversation. "Though it is similar to Reiki, the blessing is actually a gift of divine grace. The Divine – whatever you perceive that to be: Jesus, Buddha, Krishna, the universe, higher intelligence, whatever you like to call it – has intervened, giving us what we could not strive to achieve through our own efforts. The blessing allows us to rediscover that we are all part of the collective consciousness, that we are not separate from one other, we are one," Rajesh continued, moving his hands expressively, as though to orchestrate his words. "The mind, which is a very ancient mind, has created the illusion that we are all separate from each other, causing conflict and isolation. From this illusion arises the belief that we must fight for our survival, at the expense of all others, and even the planet." He paused for a moment, letting his words sink in before taking up his theme, again. "Man is the only creature who has lost touch with the reality of collective consciousness. Birds know this connection; it stirs them to migrate to warmer climates at the right moment. Fish know this, also; they swim in their shoals, weaving an intricate dance that is neither taught nor learned but is an integral part of their being."

"Yes, yes!" trilled Daphne, interrupting again and Rajesh, who seemed to have infinite patience, folded his hands in his lap, waiting for her to continue. "It's like the Tsunami. My friend was in Thailand just before it struck. She's a psychic, like me, and really in tune with the universe. She told me she remembered, that morning, that there was a strange silence in the air and that no birds were singing. They'd gone down to the beach but, as soon as she went in the water, she said she could sense some kind of vibration. She didn't know what it was but she sensed it was bad, so she packed up the whole family and they left as soon as they could." Daphne paused dramatically before delivering her closing vignette, "The whole resort was destroyed when the wave struck. They were one of the few families to survive."

"It's strange," commented John, "I read that when they were clearing the beaches they found very few corpses of animals or fishes. It was almost as though they knew…"

The discussion was interrupted by yet another yawn, distracting John from his theme. Turning instinctively towards the noise, he was greeted by the sight of Rod with his mouth open so wide that his jaw seemed in danger of dislocating. The memory of a hippopotamus he had glimpsed at a watering hole on safari in Kenya that year flashed vividly into his mind.

Lily could feel a sense of anger rising up in her chest and thought she would have to put her fist in her mouth to stop herself from screaming. She must be sitting in the presence of two of the rudest people in the world: Rod, who had absolutely no manners or empathy and Daphne, who clearly thought she was the most important person on the planet! The thought of the next few days in their company, coupled with Marcie's thinly-disguised contempt, made her feel quite exhausted. She didn't know if she would be able to make it through the next few days without large quantities of red wine. At least she still had chocolate in her suitcase which was some consolation.

Rajesh was speaking again. Lily dragged herself back from her private hell and tried to focus on his words.

"There is much more that can be said about the blessing and Oneness, but we have several more days to continue our discussions. What I would like you to do now is prepare yourself for your first blessing. Once you have experienced it, things will becomeclearer. Please close your eyes." The guide's voice continued, melodious and soothing. "Now concentrate on your breathing, long and deep, and relax. After I have placed my hands on your head, you may lie down for a few moments to allow the process towork effectively. We will now begin."

Lily felt a little bit nervous. She'd seen Holy Rollers receiving what they called Laying on of Hands at the Pentecostal church her grandparents used to take her to when she was staying with them. She remembered being terrified, at the age of about five, seeing the demented-looking preacher pacing up and down the aisles, pouncing on members of the congregation. Grabbing their heads and performing what looked like a vigorous shampooing, he would bellow, "Demons come out! Demons come out!" The supposedly afflicted person would then throw himself on the floor and flail around, wailing. Lily was quite sure she had a number of metaphorical demons that could do with exorcising but she would prefer not to be delivered in that manner. Her bout of nervousness was becoming more acute; Rajesh was certainly silent on his feet and she didn't know where he was. She wouldn't want to put the guide in the same category as a mosquito but it felt like a similar scenario; if there was one in the room, you'd rather know where it was.

Then Rajesh's hand descended gently on to Lily's head, resting there firmly for about thirty seconds before he moved on. She felt herself flooded with a mild sense of bliss that was lovely, really lovely! She stretched herself out at the side of the couch and drifted away into a deep sense of relaxation. All her earlier irritation had gone; she couldn't even remember what she'd been annoyed about. It was better than her favourite hot stone massage. She had no idea how much time had passed when Rajesh's voice summoned her back to the present.

"Please open your eyes and sit up slowly." Reluctantly, she did so, moving as slowly as possible so that she didn't jolt herself from her bliss. Looking around the group, she could see most of them were as astonished as she was.

"Wow!" Tom exhaled, "that's like really good weed!"

Rajesh smiled at them from the front of the room. "Dinner will be served for everyone in the restaurant at eight o'clock. This evening you may wish to spend some time in solitude with your thoughts, giving your attention to whatever you are experiencing. We will all meet in the main bure at eight o'clock tomorrow morning, to listen to Ananda Giri-ji speak. Thank you." Bowing slightly, he left the lounge.

"Well. What did you think of that?" Stella asked Lily.

"It was astonishing! I really don't know what to say," answered Lily.

"I know what to say," said Rod, pushing past them. "Bunkum!"

"Insufferable man!" hissed Lily, her sense of calm beginning to wobble. "Why is he even here?"

"We're all here for a reason," replied Stella. "Though it may not be the reason we think." She looked at her watch. "Dinner's being served in ten minutes. Come on."

Meandering down the path to the restaurant, the women linked arms affectionately.

"You've had the blessing before, haven't you?" asked Lily. "You weren't surprised by the experience."

"Yes. The guides have been here since last week so that they could meditate and prepare. I came over to help them settle in; they gave me several blessings while I was with them. It can be different every time. Sometimes it's like a sense of bliss."

"That's what I felt!" exclaimed Lily. Her friend nodded. "Sometimes I felt so happy that I just couldn't help laughing out loud. And once or twice I felt such a profound sense of peace that my mind became completely still."

They walked on in silence for a few minutes, enjoying the warm breeze that blew in from the ocean.

A little way ahead, Tom and Gina strolled hand in hand. Their laughter drifted back to Stella and Lily as Tom bent his head to whisper something to his wife. She squealed with outraged delight, slapping him on the arm. Tom reached up and, plucking a frangipani flower from a low-hanging branch, tucked it behind her ear. Gina stood on tiptoes to kiss her husband and they strolled on.

The touching scene made Lily's heart contract. It was just too poignant, the epitome of everything that had been missing in her marriage to Matt. Suddenly, she felt she needed to be alone.

"Stella," she paused, "I don't really feel hungry. I think I'm going to do what Rajesh suggested and spend some time on my own. I think I'll take a walk on the beach. Do you mind?"

"Of course not," Stella assured her. "It's a good idea. The blessing brings a lot of things to the surface. It's good to take the time to let the experience sink in. I'll see you back at the bure."

"OK." Lily gave her friend a grateful hug and started to make her way down the narrow path that wound its way towards the ocean.

Chapter 6

As she reached the sand, Lily took off her shoes, leaving them at the foot of a young palm tree.

"It shouldn't be hard to find you again," she said to it, placing her hand on the rough trunk. "You're the smallest in your class, like me."

She headed West along the beach, intending to walk to the lighthouse. The tide was way out and there was little chance of her being cut off. She walked along the wet sand, her toes sinking into its substance with that delicious sensation she remembered from holidays in Cornwall when she was a little girl. She was being very nostalgic all of a sudden, reminiscing about her childhood, her marriage. Why had it upset her so much to see Tom and Gina so happy? It wasn't that she was jealous; she wished them every happiness. And why had it come up now? She sighed, having no clear answers to her questions.

Looking across the expanse of water, she could make out flashing lights just above the horizon. Stopping, she peered into the dusk. It must be a private jet landing at Pele. Her thoughts drifted back to the afternoon they had arrived on the island. At the airport, Stella had said something about the blessing process bringing up unresolved issues. Perhaps that was happening to her.

She continued walking, matching the flow of the ocean, her footsteps rising and falling with the rhythm of the waves. The combined effect was subtly hypnotic and Lily felt herself fall into a kind of trance. She moved slowly along the shore, her marriage playing out in her mind like a movie.

Not long after the honeymoon, it became clear that she and Matt had different ideas of what a marriage was about. In Lily's mind, when she said her wedding vows she was declaring that Matt was the most important person in her life and she would do whatever was necessary to make that her highest priority in their life together. She soon realised that Matt's expectations were different. He relaxed into comfortable familiarity, making less and less effort to socialise or spend time with her family (which was, admittedly something of a challenge).

"You go on your own," became his habitual reply to any tentative request she might make to accept an invitation to dinner, or a party. "You love socialising but you know I find it a drag after a busy week; I'd only spoil your fun." He was right. When he went with her he did spoil her fun, constantly looking at his watch, making no effort to join in the conversation and staring broodingly into the middle distance. As nine-thirty approached, (the usual time that Matt's tolerance for such events ran out) she could feel herself becoming increasingly tense, hoping that he wouldn't demand abruptly that they leave and offend yet another host. She realised that her social life had become one long nightmare of damage limitation and had eventually accepted defeat, leaving Matt to watch whatever unmissable match was on the sports channel.

She couldn't understand what had happened to the charming, witty man she had married. He had always been so much fun and seemed to have everything in life that he could want. His career as a sports journalist had really taken off; all the long hours and early mornings had been worth the effort, landing him a coveted position on the weekend sports revue. He had laughed, saying that he had a charmed life, that everything he had ever wanted came to him with little effort. Maybe that was the problem: things came to him too easily. Lily knew that she certainly hadn't put up any resistance to his charms; they'd moved in together after six months and were engaged within a year, Matt presenting her with a beautiful tanzanite ring, her favourite stone. They'd married in June of the following year, a day so perfect its memory still made her smile.

At Christmas she'd bumped into an old friend at the office. Her magazine shared the premises with one of the monthly glossies that hired Diana for the occasional freelance article. She greeted Lily with an exuberant hug.

"Darling, you look wonderful! Married life must be treating you well! Oh, no! What have I said?" she gasped, mortified, as tears coursed down her friend's face.

"Diana, I'm so tired of putting on a brave face," sniffed Lily, "I think it was a mistake to marry Matt. He seems so different since we got married, I just don't know him any more."

Her friend steered her to a quiet corner of the canteen, insisted that she sit down and returned a few minutes later with two cups of tea and a plate of chocolate biscuits.

"Now," she said kindly, "tell me exactly what that husband of yours has been getting up to."

"Oh, I don't know. He just doesn't want to do anything any more. He says he's tired and doesn't have the energy to go out at the moment. I do everything on my own. I'm living with another person and I've never been lonelier."

"Has it been going on long?"

Lily nodded ruefully, "Months."

"So, what does the doctor say?"

Her friend threw up her hands. "Don't even go there! I suggested he might be depressed and maybe he should make an appointment at the surgery but he went mad. Accused me of being over-reactive and that I was the one who needed to see the doctor."

Diana frowned. "The trouble with Matt is that he's very bright and very spoiled. He's never had to work hard for anything and likes to have his own way. Don't let him manipulate you into thinking that you're expecting too much from him. Write him a letter and tell him how you're feeling; that way he won't be able to argue his way out of listening to what you have to say."

Lily gave her a watery smile. "Thanks, Diana. Just having someone to talk to has made me feel so much better."

"You're welcome." Diana squeezed her hand. "Let me know how you get on."

Lily had left her letter for Matt to find when he came home the following evening, while she was at her Pilates class. She wanted him to have some time to absorb what she had written before they saw each other. She put her key in the lock with some trepidation later that evening but, as she opened the front door, he swept her off her feet in a bear-hug and kissed her neck.

"Darling, I'm so sorry, I've been a fool," he murmured in her ear. "Quick! Go and get ready, I've got a table booked at Gian-Luca's in half an hour."

Wreathed in smiles, Lily ran up the stairs to shower and get changed, so happy she was able to forgive her husband's clichéd apology. Come to think of it, he hadn't really apologised at all, just pulled a line from every cheesy movie that had ever been made. Her mother's voice echoed in her mind. 'Charm without substance is like the froth on a cappuccino: aesthetically pleasing but serves no useful purpose and quickly dissolves.' She brushed away the thought; she was being unfair. He had said he was sorry and she would give him a chance to prove it.

The next few weeks were idyllic. Matt took her on a surprise trip to Venice, lavished flowers and her favourite chocolates on her and generally treated Lily like a princess. Then the excuses started again and, little by little, he returned to his lethargy. Whenever he sensed Lily was becoming too disgruntled, he would surprise her with a carefully-chosen gift or a trip to the theatre. This saddened her more than ever as she realised these gestures were like patches of blue sky among perpetual rain clouds. She lived in constant hope that the weather would take a permanent change for the better but it was like trying to wish a Caribbean climate on Scunthorpe. She had thrown herself into her work, spending more and more time at the magazine's offices. She had come up with the idea of an online forum for teenagers, where she not only offered them advice about boyfriends and careers but they could share their own experiences and create their own peer group to support each other. It had been the first of its kind and a great success, rewarding Lily with the offer of promotion to Deputy Editor at the magazine. She had accepted on the condition that she retained her role on the forum, not wanting to lose contact with the teenagers.

Her new job helped distract her from home life and things had continued in the same way for the next few months. That October, a card had arrived in the post, inviting them to their friend Josh's fortieth birthday weekend. It was being held at a Landmark Trust property in Scotland and the majority of their friends had been invited. Lily broached the subject over dinner, not really expecting Matt to show any enthusiasm. True to form, he rolled his eyes in disdain.

"Spend the weekend in a draughty old castle in Scotland, I should think not! And you know I can't bear Charlotte. She's such a bore."

"But she's Josh's wife and he was your best man. We were expecting this invitation, anyway; how are you going to explain not being there?"

"I'm sure you'll think of something," he replied nonchalantly, returning to the sports page.

"Actually, I won't," Lily's tone was icy. "I'm sick and tired of always making excuses for you. You haven't made an effort with our friends for months. I'm sure they think I've hit you over the head and stuffed your body down the well ... which is starting to look like an attractive option," she muttered, getting up from the table.

"Not the same old record again!" groaned Matt in exasperation. "Our friends understand that I have a demanding job and can't go running about all over the country at the drop of a hat. I wish you could be half as understanding. I didn't think, when I married you, that you would be such a baby about going to places on your own."

"And I didn't think, when I married you, that I would be so completely alone!" retorted Lily, slamming out of the kitchen.

Three weeks later, defiantly, she took the flight to Inverness, though the last thing she felt like doing was socialising. The atmosphere at home was decidedly strained and neither she nor Matt had made an effort to make things better. Lily felt weary to her core. She was tired of living in hope that things would get better. As much as it baffled her to think that Matt wanted such an empty sham of a marriage, she could see now that he did. All he required in a partner was that she was easy on the eye and bright enough to trot out at the occasional work functions he needed to attend. She had to be independent enough to look after herself and keep up their social life single-handed, preserving the myth that he was a fun-loving, likeable guy, just sadly over-worked. Other than that, she could be inter-changeable with any female. It was a role that no longer held any attraction for her.

Watching the mist swirling around the airport as they made their final approach, Lily felt it was a metaphor for her life. She knew she should get out of the dense mist but it was too thick for her to find her way. She didn't want to continue to wander about aimlessly; she needed some help to guide her out.

Josh was waiting for her in the arrivals hall, just as he'd promised. Seeing six-foot-four of solid reliability caused her to lose the tight rein she'd held on her emotions. Dropping her case at his feet, she flung her arms around him, burying her face in his chest to hide her tears. Patting her back absent-mindedly Josh repeated his usual greeting.

"Hello, Little One. What's the weather like down there?"

"Dear Josh," smiled Lily through her tears, "you're always the same."

"Well, who else would I be?" he laughed. "Come on, let's go and join the party."

They drove quietly for a while, Lily relishing the familiarity of an old friend who wasn't made uncomfortable by silence. She was grateful that Josh hadn't questioned her about her swollen eyes. She just needed a little respite from the discourse that was repeated over and over in her head. Anyway, this was Josh's weekend and she wouldn't spoil it by doing a 'poor me' routine. Following the twists and turns of the narrow country roads flanked by beech hedges, she was lulled into a false sense of being in a maze. Another metaphor for her life, like the mist. "OK, OK," she muttered to the universe, "I get the message."

"What's that, Sweetie?"

"Nothing, Josh, just a moment of madness."

"Well, we all have those," he observed, cheerfully. "Here we are." Sweeping round a final bend, he turned into the driveway of what could only be described as a small castle.

"Goodness, Josh!" gasped Lily. "You've surpassed yourself this time!"

"It's rather lovely, isn't it?" he chuckled. "Oops! Mind the sheep!" He swerved to avoid some ewes that had chosen exactly the wrong moment to dash across the drive. "The estate grazes them on the grounds, saves them from mowing all that grass. What was I saying?" He rubbed his chin absent-mindedly. "Oh, yes! The castle. Charlotte found it. She's rather good at that sort of thing. Come on, let's get you indoors and unpacked. There are still a few folk to arrive, so I'll be doing the airport run for most of the afternoon, but we'll meet in the billiard room for drinks at seven. Take some time to relax until then. Charlotte's given you the room with the claw-foot bath; she thought you'd like that."

"You're both lovely, you know that?" Lily gazed up at him

adoringly.

"Well, well. Very kind," muttered the gentle giant, flushing faintly pink.

At ten past seven, Lily swaggered down the elegant staircase and paused dramatically at the bottom, leaning against the banister.

"Mr Deville," she drawled, 'I'm ready for my close-up." Giggling, she tip-tapped across the majestic entrance hall in the new Christian Louboutin's she had bought for the occasion and headed towards the billiard room. She was feeling in much better spirits. Charlotte had popped her head around the door earlier on, while she was unpacking, and presented her with a chilled bottle of Veuve Clicquot.

"Oooh! How decadent!"

"Absolutely," agreed Charlotte, "and it's to be enjoyed in the bath."

"You're really spoiling us," said Lily, gratefully.

"Well, this is the party we would have liked to have thrown when we got married, but we were still impoverished students. But don't tell everyone I brought you a bottle of Veuve; the rest of them only got Lanson. See you at seven," winked Charlotte, hurrying off to see her other guests.

After a number of glasses of good champagne and a luxurious soak in the biggest bath Lily had ever seen, her stress had begun to fade away. As she opened the door to the billiard room, she was ready to enjoy the evening. Josh and Charlotte always threw such good parties.

"There you are, darling," called her hostess, seeing her enter the room. "Come over and join us. Lovely Lou-Lous," she said, observing her friend's feet. "New?"

"Yes," nodded Lily, feeling a frisson of guilt. "I'm such a hypocrite. I spend all my time telling teenage girls not to waste money on designer labels. It's a good thing they can't see my shoe collection."

"Well, as we all have to wear clothes, they might as well be as gorgeous as possible. Talking of gorgeous, this is George, Josh's new golfing friend."

George was indeed gorgeous; not a conventional Adonis, being a slight five-foot-seven with mousy brown hair, but he had seductive green eyes and a smile that could melt an iceberg. He was also very much at ease with himself without being arrogant – always an attractive trait in a man.

"Golf!" Lily threw down the gauntlet. "It always seems such a pity to ruin a pleasant walk."

George laughed amicably. "Golf widow, are you?"

"I am," Lily nodded solemnly. "In fact," she said, warming to her theme, "I'm the quintessential sports widow. Any time there is a major sporting event, be it live or on television, I must venture out alone. In fact, some of my newer friends have never met my husband and are starting to believe he's a figment of my imagination." She smiled brightly. "I need more champagne."

"Oh dear," she lamented to Charlotte, watching George weave across the room to replenish their glasses, "I was starting to rant."

"Only a very little," her friend reassured her, patting her arm. "I'm surprised you haven't indulged sooner, considering what you have to put up with from that silly husband of yours. You don't always have to observe social protocol and pretend that everything's fine, you know," she continued. "We all know Matt's an arse. Josh told him as much when he saw him at the club last week."

"Matt saw Josh at the club?"

"He didn't tell you?" Charlotte raised an eyebrow. "Well, I'm not surprised. Josh gave him quite a dressing-down from what I gather. He may not be the most eloquent man in the world but he's very fond of you. Doesn't like the way Matt's been behaving. Told him if he didn't pull his socks up, he'd lose you."

"Fancy Old Josh being so astute," said Lily, her voice betraying a hint of dejection.

"So, it's come to that?" Her friend looked at her sadly.

"Yes...No...I don't know! Let's not talk about it now, George's coming back." Fixing a brilliant smile to her face, she took her glass of champagne from George's outstretched hand. "Oooh, lovely!"

Charlotte sat Lily next to George at dinner, whispering that she thought it would do her the world of good to indulge in some outrageous flirting.

Why not? thought Lily. It had been a while since an attractive man had paid her some attention. She entered into the dance of flirtation: advancing and withdrawing, flattering and receiving flattery. It was most enjoyable – an illusion but a pleasant one. As the evening progressed, she forgot her troubles and found herself enjoying George's company more and more. He was attentive and witty, entertaining her with amusing stories and laughing at her jokes. The perfect companion.

The evening improved still further when Josh tapped his glass, announcing that the DJ had finished setting up in the ballroom.

"Let the dancing commence!" commanded their host.

"Come on, Lily! Let's show them how it's done," grinned George, pulling her to her feet.

Always delighted to have the opportunity to dance, Lily still had a brief moment of reticence about taking to the floor with an ex- public-schoolboy. They all seemed to share the disconcerting characteristic of dancing like Thunderbird puppets who'd had their strings cut. She needn't have worried; George was a sublime dancer, a strong male partner who spun her expertly around the floor, feeling the rhythm of the music, flowing with the changes in tempo. She felt like a contestant on Strictly Come Dancing, she hadn't had so much fun in ages. After dancing for what seemed like a few minutes, she looked at her watch and saw that it was 1:40 a.m.

"George, I need some water."

"Me too. Let's get some fresh air." Taking her hand, George guided her from the dance-floor and, grabbing a bottle of water from the drinks table, led her through the open French windows, on to the terrace.

It was a clear, still night, the sky hung with innumerable stars; it looked like a sorcerer's cloak, diamonds on deep blue velvet.

"Look, there's Orion's Belt," said George, pointing out the constellation, "and there – the Seven Sisters." Lily shivered, not sure if it was the chill of the night air or George's presence as he stood close behind her, shielding her from the wind that whipped across the grounds of the old castle.

"You're cold. I don't have my jacket."

Lily reached back, took hold of George's wrists and wrapped his arms around her, leaning against his chest. He rested his chin on her shoulder and they stood in silence, contemplating the dramatic expanse of sky that spread out over the shrouded landscape.

"When I look at the stars like this, it always makes me realise how tiny and insignificant my problems are," Lily sighed. "They've been shining for millions of years and will still be shining millions of years after I've left this planet."

"Very philosophical," replied George," and it's good to have an elevated perspective at times but let me say, just for the record, your husband is a damn fool! Any man that doesn't want to be with such a funny, interesting, beautiful woman deserves to lose her. If you were my wife, I wouldn't let you out of my sight."

Lily felt her stomach flip over. She was suddenly aware of how much she'd needed to feel desired and appreciated. George turned her round gently, tilted her chin and kissed her purposefully on the mouth. She returned the passion of his kiss, her arms twined around his neck and felt herself losing sense of her surroundings as her body began to respond to his touch.

"Mmrrr!"

"What was that? Ow!" Lily felt sudden pressure on her bottom that wasn't from George's hands.

"I don't believe it! It's a bloody ram!" George was incredulous. "Where the hell's that come from?"

"It must have wandered up from the grounds. The estate grazes a flock here, apparently."

The ram stood glaring at them with an uncannily human expression on its face, though Lily couldn't work out whether it was trying to say, "We'll have none of that here, thank you," or, "Move over, mate, she's mine!" George's expression was all too easy to read: it said, "Thanks a lot! Perfect timing!" She wasn't sure which she found more amusing. Either way, she had regained control of her sobriety.

George noticed the change in her demeanour. "That woolly bastard's ruined my chances, hasn't he?"

Lily laughed at his cheated expression, "'Fraid so. I am sorry. You're a lovely kisser."

"You're sure there's no chance of…"

"Mmrrr!" grunted the ram, advancing purposefully towards them again.

"Quick!" she giggled, grabbing George's hand and dashing for the safety of the ballroom. "He was looking at your crotch that time!"

The party was still in full swing and nobody seemed to have missed them. Turning, she smiled fondly at her companion.

"Come on. Let's have one more dance before I go to bed."

They reached the dance floor just as La Vida Loca began to

play. Lily shimmied about, twisting and gyrating, giving it every last ounce of her energy. She stopped dead on the final beat in a classic show-girl pose, arms above her head, as George dropped at her feet.

"Wow! Someone's woken up your Diva!" exclaimed Charlotte as she spun past with Josh. A wink was George's only reply.

George rose from his knees and enveloped Lily in a hug, swinging her off the floor.

"You're a wonderful girl," he murmured in her ear. "If only things were different."

"Thank you, George," she said, placing her palm against his cheek. "You've been an absolute sweetheart. I haven't had so much fun in years. Now kiss me, and say goodnight."

Closing the bedroom door behind her, Lily slipped off her shoes which were now thoroughly broken in, and climbed on to the imposing four-poster bed. As scenes from the evening ran through her mind, a smile played around her lips: amusing conversation, thoroughly ostentatious dancing … and that kiss. Lily closed her eyes and sank back into the pillows, remembering the delicious sensation of George's lips. Suddenly, she sat back up again, slamming her fists into the mattress.

"Arrghh! Damn you, Mother, for bringing me up with morals!"

Lily walked into the lounge on the following evening to find Matt in his habitual position, in front of the sports channel. She spoke his name and he reluctantly dragged his attention from the television. Seeing her resolute expression, his face became masked in sadness.

"It's over, isn't it?"

"Yes, Mattie, it is. I can't go on like this."

Switching off the TV set, he came to her and took her hands.

"I'm sorry, Lily. I just can't change. I never meant to hurt you like this; I'm just too selfish to be married."

She held his head as he wept, her own eyes curiously dry. In that moment, when everything had been said, Lily felt a sudden wave of compassion for her husband; he was what he was, and that was that.

The separation was quiet and civilised. Matt signed over the house to her and moved to an apartment in Docklands. Two years later, by mutual consent, the separation was finalised and they filed for divorce. The marriage passed away as though it had never happened; there had been so few memories of a shared life.

Lily brushed her hair from her eyes. She had walked the whole length of the beach and back without resolving her feelings. Climbing into one of the hammocks that was suspended between the palm trees, she tucked up her feet, arms behind her head and racked her brain, trying to uncover what was disturbing her. She had forgiven Matt long ago; it couldn't be that.

The tide was turning. Lying back in the hammock, Lily watched the reflection of the stars dancing across the water and let go of her turbulent thoughts, her mind falling silent. The moon reappeared from behind the clouds, casting a shimmering path across the ocean to Lily's feet. As its glow illuminated the water, her mind cleared. Yes, she had forgiven Matt for his selfish behaviour, for the long lonely evenings when they had been in the same room. Yes, she had forgiven him for making her always go out alone, enduring the pity of their friends. She had forgiven him all of this and more but she had never forgiven herself. She saw, for the first time, that she had blamed herself, had thought that somehow she had deserved to be treated that way. As this realisation dawned, Lily covered her face and wept long-overdue tears for her younger self, a woman whose only mistake was to deny her right to be loved.

Chapter 7

Arriving at the beach-front restaurant, Marcie began to scan the room.

"Look, Scott, there's that couple I told you about, the hedge-fund managers from Washington. Let's go and join them."

"Networking again?" asked Scott "I thought we'd make the most of spending time with Tom and Gina, seeing as we're not with them very often."

"Fine! If you'd rather be with them, go ahead," Marcie huffed, stomping off towards the hedge-funders. Straight away, she regretted her reaction; she half hoped that Scott would come after her but she'd been far too much of a bitch lately. He was right, she could never resist the opportunity to network but that wasn't entirely why she'd preferred to sit with strangers this evening. She'd had a very strange experience during the blessing; it was as though she was sitting on her father's lap as a little girl, safe and content without a care in the world. Coming back to the present as she'd opened her eyes, she had felt lost and vulnerable. She had forgotten what it was like to feel so cared for and she wasn't sure she wanted those memories re-awakened. It was so much easier to hide from your feelings with strangers; they didn't know a thing about you, allowing you to create whatever character you wanted to be.

Sitting down at their table, Marcie greeted the couple cheerfully. "Hi guys! Can I join you? The food looks delicious, doesn't it?" Her mask firmly back in place, she settled down for an evening of superficial pleasantries.

Scott pulled out a chair next to Gina, who looked at him quizzically. "What's up, Sweetie? Marcie not joining us?"

He pulled a face. "No, she wants to mix and mingle and got annoyed when I said I'd prefer to catch up with you guys."

"You could still go over and join them," she suggested.

"I know. And I probably should, but I just don't want to do the whole networking thing at the moment."

Gina exchanged a look with her husband but decided not to pursue the subject; Scott looked dejected enough without her pressurising him.

"So what did you think of the blessing?" he asked the couple.

Gina thought for a moment before replying. "I just felt really relaxed and contented. Like lying in a warm bath."

"Yeah, Honey, I was there with you," agreed Tom. Adjusting his glasses, he continued thoughtfully, "I'm still not sure if I think energy was really transferred or whether the suggestion that it would be acted like a placebo – but either way, the end result was pretty damn good."

"Like that weed you mentioned," Scott chuckled. "I didn't know you still smoked dope."

"Oh, I don't, not since college," Tom shook his head, "but I can still remember that sensation. No, fishing's my mood-enhancer of choice these days. But what about you, Scott? What was your experience?"

"Well …" he hesitated before replying, "I know it sounds kind of flaky, but I just felt really nice about myself." They waited for him to continue. "I actually felt like I was OK, you know?" He looked at their expressions intently, to reassure himself that they had grasped what he was trying to say. "I know everyone thinks I have a charmed life and, believe me, I know that I have, but lately everything I do seems to be slightly out of step. Marcie's an awesome girl but we just don't seem to connect at the moment. I have a great position in the firm but … I don't know, it doesn't seem to fire me up like it used to." He tried to laugh off what he had just said, adding, "I guess this is the proverbial mid-life crisis."

"And this evening?" Gina gently steered him back to his experience. "You felt good about yourself?"

"Yes," Scott was serious again, "and that everything would

work out. It's funny," he said, sounding surprised, "I didn't even know I'd been so down on myself."

"You're a great guy, Scott," she said, firmly, "but your biggest problem is that you always want to make everyone else happy. You can't. It's their job to look after their own happiness and your job to look after yours." Using the table as leverage to help her to her feet, she patted the swell of her belly.

"As I'm eating for two, I'm off to get dessert. Anyone else want some?"

The three friends walked in the direction of their *bures*, the men slowing their pace to accommodate Gina's waddle. Marcie had left the restaurant early, dropping by their table briefly before saying she had a headache and wanted to get an early night. It was quite late but Scott still wasn't ready to turn in. His thoughts were still tumbling around his head like billiard balls and he wanted to take some time to sort through them.

"Coming in for a cup of tea?" offered Gina as they reached their porch.

"No thanks." Scott kissed her cheek. "I'm going to get some fresh air."

"Night, fella," Tom shook his hand. "See you tomorrow."

Cutting through a grove of frangipani trees, Scott arrived at the beach. The moon had just begun to peer out from behind scurrying clouds that chased across the sky. He spotted some lounge chairs lined up at the end of the beach and began to head towards them.

As he approached the water's edge, the sound of someone crying reached him on the summer breeze. Loud, heart-broken sobs cut through the still air and Scott quickened his pace, fearing that someone was in trouble. As he drew closer, he identified that the sound came from a person curled up in one of the hammocks.

He stopped in his tracks; it was Lily. Unsure of how to proceed, he waited in the shadows. Though clearly very upset, she didn't seem to be injured in any way. Scott was embarrassed to have intruded upon her sorrow; maybe he should just creep away and let her grieving run its course. He hesitated; the tears seemed to be subsiding. After a few more minutes, they stopped altogether and Lily sat up, searching through her clothing to find something to wipe her eyes. Tentatively, Scott started towards her. He called her name quickly, not wanting to startle her by his sudden appearance.

"Lily, it's Scott. Please don't be embarrassed. I just wanted to know that you're OK."

He saw her silhouette freeze. After a brief pause, her voice drifted back to him.

"You really are a stalker, aren't you, Scott? Are you trying to compile a montage for *Candid Camera*?"

Reassured by her humour, he pulled up a lounge chair and sat down next to the hammock.

"Don't suppose you've got a tissue," asked Lily, painfully aware of her swollen eyes and running mascara.

"I do, as a matter of fact," Scott replied, holding out a white linen handkerchief.

"I can't use that!" exclaimed Lily, handing it back. "I need to blow my nose; it'll be ruined."

"Well, if you want to sit there looking like a banshee," he teased.

"Give that to me!" Lily snatched it back, wiped her eyes and then blew her nose loudly. "Don't say I didn't warn you," she said defiantly, holding out the soiled handkerchief.

Scott recoiled in mock horror. "Toxic waste! No thanks! You can keep it."

"Hmmm," she said, giving him a speculative look. "So what exactly were you doing, sneaking about in the bushes, anyway?

Looking for skinny dippers again?"

"Of course," he concurred. "Got my binoculars and everything. Seriously, Lily, is everything OK? You sounded pretty upset just now."

She didn't speak for a moment, staring out across the ocean. When she turned back to him her expression was bemused.

"Funnily enough, it is," she replied. "I feel really peaceful after all that crying, like I've shed an old skin." She gave an embarrassed laugh. "I know it sounds silly."

"Why would that sound silly? It sounds like you really let go of something. What was it?"

"I was thinking about my marriage," she said quietly, "and I realised I'd never really let myself grieve over it. Too busy doing all that strong, capable stuff. Anyway," she waved her hand dismissively, "you don't want to hear all that dreary stuff."

"I do, if you don't mind talking about it," he said truthfully, "especially how you resolved things."

Lily started to tell him her story, hesitating at first, convinced that he only wanted to reassure himself she had calmed down. As she accepted that his interest was genuine, she opened up, even telling him about her Norma Desmond pose and the encounter with the sheep. He interjected with occasional questions, sympathised with George's frustration and shook his head in disbelief at Matt's behaviour.

Listening to Lily's tale, Scott felt profound admiration for this woman, so strong and composed as she shared the demise of her relationship. Not once did she malign her ex-husband, although he would have said she had every right to do so. What a selfish bastard! Scott knew he would be wise to keep his opinion to himself; Lily wouldn't want to hear any recriminations about Matt. One thing was clear at least, she did seem to have found a resolution.

He couldn't contain his curiosity any longer. "Why did you

marry him? I mean, there must have been signs of trouble before the wedding."

"Of course there were," Lily agreed, "but I was determined not to see them. And he could be very sweet and charming, in the beginning. Then I got caught up with the wedding circus and with my job at the magazine there wasn't really much time to think. It's curious," she continued pensively, "I adored my dad and I always thought I'd married a man just like him, but afterwards I realised I'd married a carbon copy of my mother: charming but impossible to please and who constantly undermined me. Dad's love was a given, but I always felt that I had to earn Mum's love, and that I never quite succeeded. Funny how history repeats itself."

They sat in silence for a while, listening to the melody of the waves as they crashed against the shore, then Lily spoke again.

"So, how are things between you and Marcie? Not so good, I guess, if you're here rather than back at your *bure*."

"We had another row at the restaurant. I'm just as much to blame as her. We can't seem to be able to stop winding each other up at the moment." He held his face in his hands. "I don't know, maybe Rajesh can help us out. He certainly seems to have the juice."

"Yes, it really was an amazing experience, wasn't it?"

"It certainly was," Scott agreed, "and more of the same tomorrow. I guess we should try to get some sleep."

Lily picked up her shoes and they made their way back up the path to the *bures*. What a strange time, she thought, running over the happenings of the last couple of days. She had been through the emotional mill, experiencing every crazy feeling possible, made a wonderful friend in Stella and felt the bliss of the blessing. And Scott was so kind, making sure she was all right like that. There weren't many men who would have listened to her pouring out her heart over her marriage – unless they were gay. She considered the possibility for a moment before dismissing it. A gay man would have been more excited at the mention of her designer shoe collection.

Reaching the top of the incline, Lily stumbled over one of the coconuts that lay strewn across the path and would have fallen if Scott hadn't caught her by the arm.

"Careful!" he said, steadying her. "We don't want any accidents."

As he touched her arm, Lily felt a sense of *frisson* shiver across her skin. His hand rested longer than was necessary on her elbow and she looked up, startled. They watched each other silently for a moment before Lily pulled away.

"Sleep well, Scott," she said, walking away, "see you tomorrow."

Neither of them noticed Marcie watching them from the *bure*'s balcony. The young woman stood transfixed, observing every nuance of Scott's and Lily's body language as they stood together. Nothing had happened, she was fairly confident of that, but still her anger rose up like bile in her throat. If he'd had a quick fumble in the bushes with another woman, it would have been easier to handle than this. What she couldn't cope with was the tenderness in Scott's face as he looked at Lily – a look she hadn't seen for a long time. As Scott's key turned in the lock, she walked back into the *bure* and stood waiting for him in the dark.

"Hey, Marcie, I'm back," he whispered. "Are you awake?"

"Yes, Scott, I am," she said, turning on the light, "and we need to talk."

Chapter 8

"Hi, Sweetie," Stella tapped at Lily's bedroom door. "I thought I heard movement. I've just made a pot of peppermint tea. Want some?"

"That would be lovely, thank you," called Lily, putting down her book.

Stella returned a few moments later, carrying a tray. "Nelson brought round some fresh mango, so I cut some up for us."

"I am being spoiled!" said Lily, taking her cup of tea and a bowl of mango. "It's not my birthday, you know."

"Don't tell me you only expect to get breakfast in bed on your birthday!" Stella was astonished. "My dear, this is a delightful indulgence and should be enjoyed whenever possible." She settled herself in the chair next to Lily's bed. "What's that you're reading?"

"*The Alchemist*, Paulo Coelho," Lily held up a well-thumbed paperback. "I don't know how many times I've read it; it's like an old friend."

"It was a favourite of my husband's, his copy was even more dog-eared than that."

"I was sorry to hear about your husband," said Lily, gently. "Has it been long?"

"Seven years," replied Stella nodding. "He was a wonderful man." She smiled wistfully. "Charlie's the spitting image of him."

"It must have been hard to lose him with two small boys."

"It was heart-wrenching, I thought I'd never get over it," she agreed. "It was a brain tumour that killed him. At least it was instantaneous. The boys got me through it, children are amazingly resilient. They were, of course, devastated at first; Robert had always been so close to them. But as children do, they wept long, hard aching sobs, expressed their grief completely and then were free of it. They moved on." She paused, remembering the profound sadness she had felt at that moment in her life. "I ignored my grief, tried to be brave, keep busy but it was destroying me; I couldn't eat, couldn't sleep, to be honest I didn't really want to live. He was my soul-mate, you see."

"How did you get through it?" Lily asked.

"It was Charlie," Stella replied. "He came into my room one afternoon, when I'd gone to lie down with a headache. Perching on the edge of the bed, he said in his most grown- up voice, 'Mummy, I think you need to have a really good cry. Now, I know you think it will upset me, so I'm going to leave you to do it on your own.' With that, he took himself off and shut the door behind him. Can you imagine? A seven-year-old boy!" said Stella in wonder. "I felt as though I'd had a visitation from his father. I realised that I hadn't been brave at all; until then, I hadn't had the courage to face my loss. I cried all afternoon, howled, beat the pillows, swore at God. Everything. At the end of it all, I felt a deep sense of peace; I understood how lucky I'd been to have those precious years with Robert, some people search all their lives without finding that," she smiled. "So I wrote him a letter, remembering all the wonderful moments we'd shared in the ten years we spent together, told him how much I'd always love him, then let him go." She was thoughtful for a moment. "I still have such a sense of him being in our lives, but I don't need to cling to the past anymore."

Lily reached across to her bedside table and grabbed the box of tissues. She took one for herself then handed the box to Stella who had tears in her eyes, too.

"What did you do with the letter?" asked Lily, wiping her eyes.

"It's at my solicitor's, with my Will," said Stella. "I thought that when the boys are older they would like to know how much their parents loved each other."

"You've turned a tragedy into something beautiful," said Lily, solemnly. "I think you're very brave."

Stella shrugged. "Not particularly, I was being a terrible coward. It was Charlie's faith in me that made me brave; he knew I could make it. I suppose we'll always stretch ourselves further for those we really love than we do for ourselves."

They ate their mango in silence for a while before Stella spoke again.

"You're deep in thought. I hope I haven't upset you."

"No, not at all," Lily reassured her. "I was just thinking about what you said about really feeling your grief. A similar thing happened to me last night. I realised I'd never allowed myself to grieve for my marriage. Last night I did; I had a good weep and now I feel as though that chapter's finally closed. I'd been carrying the pain around for the last couple of years, trying to ignore it."

"Ananda Giri says that most of us have degrees in sorrow management. We're terrified of really feeling our suffering, so we spend our time trying to ignore it or manage it but, each time we push it away, the emotional charge attached to it just increases. If we ignore it long enough it comes out in other ways like comfort-eating or eventually sickness." She took Lily's empty bowl from her. "He says if we could be in the habit of really experiencing our painful emotions they would dissolve and we would be much less fearful and insecure. We'd be a lot healthier, too. As the doctors say, ninety percent of all modern diseases are caused by stress."

Lily handed Stella her cup. "Interesting in theory but not easy to do. The thought of feeling that kind of pain on a regular basis fills me with dread."

"Yes," agreed Stella, "but think how good you felt afterwards. And the reason that the feelings were so intense was that you'd been suppressing them for so long."

"Hmm. I can see what you're saying."

Stella stood up with the tray. "Part of the trouble is that society has conditioned us into thinking it's bad to feel angry or jealous or depressed, that it's not acceptable. The thing is, we will always have these facets to our personalities and the sooner we accept them, the more at ease we'll be with ourselves."

Lily grinned at her from the bed, "You're very philosophical this morning."

"I told you, I am many-faceted," Stella retorted. "Philosopher now, bitch later. I embrace all possibilities. You'd better jump in the shower while I wash up. We don't want to be late for Ananda Giri."

The meeting hall was buzzing with chatter as Lily and Stella arrived. There were a few people outside the *bure* talking on their mobile phones, giving instructions to far-flung secretaries or tapping out emails on their keypads.

"Monday morning," smiled Stella. "It's not easy to get off the hamster-wheel!"

Inside, people were mixing and mingling, saying their good mornings, waiting for the guides to arrive.

"Look, there are Tom and Gina," said Stella, heading in their direction. Lily followed reluctantly. Scott was with them and he looked as though he hadn't had much sleep. There was no sign of Marcie. Lily scanned the room; no, she wasn't there. Lily wondered if she'd been awake when Scott got back last night.

"Hi!" said Gina, greeting Lily warmly. "You're looking lovely."

"Thanks, Gina," said Lily, as they exchanged kisses, "and you're looking like a flower in bloom."

"She always does when she's pregnant," added Tom, giving Lily a hug. "I think she should be pregnant all the time."

"Easy, Honey," laughed his wife, "five are going to be plenty."

"I don't know … I like the idea of travelling about in the family bus."

"That's just the old hippie in you. He was born too late for Woodstock," she confided to Lily.

Stella and Scott were deep in conversation. He was shaking his head in response to something she had asked him, his expression perplexed. Lily couldn't hear his reply but Stella was looking incredulous. Something must have happened. Her heart sank. Maybe Marcie had seen them together last night. It was all perfectly innocent but she could understand Marcie misunderstanding the situation. Thankfully, she didn't know how Lily had felt when Scott touched her arm. She shook herself impatiently; she'd successfully avoided thinking about that scenario last night and certainly wasn't going to explore it now. It would be better to keep out of Scott's way for the moment. Excusing herself, she went to say good morning to Brenda and John.

Brenda smiled hello but, as usual, left the conversation up to John. He asked Lily for her opinion of yesterday's group meeting and agreed that it was very interesting, if somewhat outside their usual experience.

"We're from a Catholic background so it's all quite new to us," he said. "We're keeping an open mind. So far, everything Rajesh has said makes a lot of sense."

"The blessing was lovely," said Brenda, shyly. "I'm looking forward to the next one."

The guides entered the room and the people that were still standing took their seats. Raksith asked everyone to close their eyes in a few moments of quiet contemplation before Ananda Giri arrived. The lilting music filled the room and Lily felt the same calm wash over her that she had experienced during yesterday's blessing. The track continued to play for the next few minutes then faded gently. She opened her eyes to see a small Indian man, sitting cross-legged in an armchair draped in white, at the centre of the stage.

"Good morning, I am Ananda Giri. I bring you greetings from Sri Amma Bhagavan, the founders of the Oneness University in India. They are very happy that you have travelled to Pele this week to hear their message. This is a very auspicious occasion." He paused for a long moment before continuing.

"The purpose of life is to be happy, which is our natural state. Our natural state is to be aware that we are all connected to one another, to everything in the universe and be in a state of harmony. We have forgotten this state of existence. We no longer perceive that we are one. We no longer understand that there is a collective consciousness and our every action affects this consciousness as a whole." The young teacher's gaze travelled around the room.

"Man began to see himself as a separate entity, apart from the rest of the universe, apart from his fellow men and this is where conflict came into the world. If he was separate, he needed to protect himself from others in order to survive. This division has grown over the centuries and man has, for the most part, forgotten his source. In this struggle to survive, each faction has developed his own set of rules. These rules, ideals and faiths, far from being the answer to mankind's problems, are actually creating the divisions that are threatening its survival." Everyone in the room waited in anticipation for Ananda Giri to continue speaking. "Partial solutions of any kind – scientific, religious, political, economic – can no longer ensure mankind its survival. The answers provided by any groups must always be partial, limited and have limited results."

"With modern technology, the world has become small. Man is no longer individual, separate. What affects the few affects all mankind. There is no escape or avoidance of the problem, no withdrawing from the totality of the human predicament."

"One can see in all social structures the destructive effect of fragmentation taking place; nation against nation, one group against another group, one family against another family, one individual against another – religiously, socially and economically. Our very thinking is separative. It is only during times of crisis or disaster that we come together and support each other; when these moments are over, we return to our usual behaviour."

Ananda Giri held the room captivated. Though his message was compelling, it was his presence that held their attention. Lily thought she had never heard such a commanding speaker; he didn't use any clever techniques or props, he just sat crossed-legged in his chair and spoke. Each phrase was considered and measured, each word held a depth of passion and commitment that arrested her. She felt as though she was sitting in the presence of a great master like Mahatma Gandhi or Martin Luther King. Normally she wrote copious notes at meetings or seminars but gradually she stopped writing and gave this young man her full attention; she didn't want to miss a single word of what he was saying.

"How can we resolve this problem?" he continued. "Throughout the centuries, mankind has striven to find a solution to the world's conflict by his own means but with little result. It is clear that we are incapable of finding a solution on our own, which is why grace has intervened. This grace arises out of the collective consciousness. It is only by an act of grace that we can see each other as we truly are, without prejudice, without the filters of our cultural and social conditioning, without reaction from our past experiences. The blessing comes to us through this act of grace; it is the blessing process that allows us to be free of our sense of separation and return to a state of Oneness."

The room was silent. Ananda Giri sat quietly, regarding his audience. Eventually he spoke again.

"The guides will now give you an intent blessing. They will focus their attention on each person here, experiencing his heart flowering and opening up to Oneness." The guides filed on to the stage, quietly waiting for Ananda Giri to finish. "Please close your eyes and allow yourselves to receive the blessing."

The same gentle music began to play in the background as Lily closed her eyes. She felt a slight sense of anti-climax; she had been hoping to have the experience by Rajesh placing his hands on her head again. Transferring energy by intention sounded a bit like the Jedi mind meld. She sat with her eyes closed, waiting for the session to finish. Only a few seconds had passed when the same gentle sense of well-being that she had felt yesterday washed over her. She felt her shoulders relax and sank into the experience, drifting off on a wave of calm.

When Raksith began to speak from the stage, she was peeved to have her reverie interrupted. Reluctantly, she opened her eyes and focused on what the guide was saying.

"…will resume this afternoon at three o'clock, in the same location. Namaste." He held his palms together in front of his chest in a gesture of respect, then joined the other guides and they left the room.

"I'm surprised they rushed us through the blessing like that," said Lily, turning to John.

"That was twenty minutes," he said, pointing at his watch.

"I had no idea," she said, looking at the time in surprise. Lily looked around the room and saw that a lot of people were still experiencing the sensation of the blessing. Some people were already on their feet and leaving the room but most were still sitting in their chairs, in no rush to go anywhere. Looking past John, Lily could see that Brenda still had her eyes closed, in a state of complete relaxation. She smiled at John. "You might have a job moving her at the moment."

"I'm not even going to try," he smiled back.

Leaving the hall, Lily joined Stella who was chatting to Tom.

"There you are!" exclaimed Stella. "We were just talking about you. As we've got a few hours before our group session this afternoon, we thought we'd take a boat out and have a picnic lunch on board."

"It's great to see the island from the water," said Tom. "We could moor at Boatman's Cove and go snorkelling."

"What a lovely idea!" Lily agreed enthusiastically. "How long have I got to go and grab my bikini?"

"Half an hour," Stella replied. "Scott's gone to see if he can persuade Marcie to come along – apparently they had an awful row last night – and Gina's gone to organise lunch with the kitchen, so we shouldn't need any longer than that."

Agreeing to meet the rest of the party down at the quay, Stella and Lily headed back to their *bure*.

"OK, what's up?" said Stella as they walked.

"What do you mean, 'what's up'?" Lily replied, without catching her friend's eye.

"You didn't sit with us during the meeting and then your face dropped like a stone when Tom said Scott and Marcie were coming on the boat," Stella replied.

"You know that Marcie doesn't like me," said Lily. "I'm not keen on the idea of being trapped on a boat with her for a couple of hours."

"Oh, it will be fine! Marcie's a bit spiky but she'll be fine once she's out having a bit of fun."

Lily wasn't so sure but she thought she'd keep quiet. Stella didn't seem to know that she'd been with Scott last night and she didn't feel like explaining why she was so reticent about spending time with the couple. She'd done nothing wrong, after all, she mused; maybe it wouldn't be a bad thing for them to enjoy the boat together. It might put things back into perspective.

Grabbing their swimwear, hats and sun-block, the women headed down to the quay to find that there were only three people waiting for them.

"So, Marcie's not coming," said Stella as they joined the group.

"No," said Scott. "She still has a migraine."

"Come on guys. Let's get loaded up." Tom started picking up the cool-box and climbed into the boat.

"He's getting his captain's head on," grinned Gina. "Better hurry up or he might make us walk the plank."

Lily picked up her bag and stepped aboard, with Tom steadying her. She felt a huge sense of relief that Marcie wouldn't be joining them. She had been prepared to do all that she could to be pleasant to the girl and try to enjoy the afternoon as much as possible, but now she wouldn't have to. It would be really lovely just to relax and enjoy the company of her new friends. She was sure that what had passed between her and Scott was only the intensity of the moment, brought on by sharing the intimate details of her life. Lily's whole outlook had changed in a matter of moments and she felt that it was going to be a wonderful day.

Scott was also glad that Marcie had decided not to come out on the boat with them. He'd felt the full force of her wrath last night and was relieved to have some breathing space from all the drama.

When he'd arrived back from the beach, he could tell she was furious by the tension in her shoulders. He'd asked her what was wrong but she had just stood looking at Scott calmly, without saying a word. He knew what was coming next. This was her favoured technique for making an opening address in Court and he had seen her use it many times. He felt strangely absent from the scenario as she began to expound her grievances, starting with her anger that Scott had been on the beach with Lily when he could have been with her.

"I didn't go to the beach with Lily. I found her there, crying, and I just wanted to make sure she was OK. And you told me you had a migraine and were going to bed," said Scott in a tired voice. "Nothing happened."

"Oh, I know that! If I thought otherwise we wouldn't be having this conversation," snapped Marcie. "But I know what a soft touch you are for underdogs. You constantly fall short of achieving your full potential by getting caught up in some sort of cause."

Scott was bewildered. "I don't know what you're talking about."

"We're supposed to be here to meet people who would benefit our relationship. That English woman is of no interest to us but you decide to waste your time talking to her when you could be making some good business contacts. It was the same when your father organised the competition to donate equipment to the college that had the greatest improvement in its grade-point average," she continued, exasperated. "Instead of taking advantage of an outstanding PR opportunity, you started getting involved with setting up sports programmes for kids from the wrong side of town. Kids that nobody was interested in."

Scott could feel anger rising in his throat and almost choking him; the coaching of those children had been one of the recent highlights of his life and she was mocking it as though it meant nothing.

"A couple of those kids won sports scholarships to college. It gave them a sense of worth that they'd never had because no-one had believed in them before. Their grades improved radically, too. It was one of the most worthwhile things I've ever done," he said, the anger making his voice tremble.

"Yes, yes," Marcie waved away his argument. "That's all very nice but it didn't exactly further your career."

"You are unbelievable, Marcie," he replied. "In case you haven't noticed, there is absolutely nothing I need to do to further my career."

"That's exactly what I mean! You have lost all your ambition. You're just marking time to take over the business when your father dies," Marcie snapped back. "No drive, no ambition. I want to start a family in two years' time and, at the moment, you're not exactly looking like the man I want to father my children."

"It might have slipped your notice, Marcie, but I haven't asked to be your sperm donor." His voice was cold enough to freeze water. "And I'm not likely to."

Marcie had crossed the line when she talked about Scott's father dying. Though he had started to think it might not be his ambition to take over the company, he had the greatest respect for his father and even greater love. Scott worked hard in his marketing position in the firm, regularly putting in long hours; he had never used the fact that he was the president's son to get an easy ride.

Marcie knew she'd gone too far. They'd had their share of rows over the years, as all couples do, but she'd never seen him so cold and detached. He was looking at her as though he'd never seen her before in his life and found her utterly repellent. She knew she had to do something to turn the situation around and promptly burst into tears.

"Did you forget that I know you can cry on demand, Marcie?" Scott's voice was weary now, as though he was utterly tired of the whole situation. She quelled her tears and sat down on the bed, looking scared.

"I'm sorry. I just wish you would stretch yourself more," she said apologetically. "I only want you to have the success you're capable of."

"You want me to be someone I'm not," said Scott sadly, "and I can't do it any more."

"What are we going to do?" whispered Marcie, genuine tears welling in her eyes. In reply, Scott crossed the room and, sitting on the bed, pulled her into his arms.

"I'm sorry," he said, gently rocking her as the tears began to flow in earnest.

Chapter 9

The yacht was soon under way. Tom said that he and Scott would sort out the sailing between them as they weren't going far; the girls could go and sun themselves. This was the usual arrangement, Stella informed Lily; she and Gina had perfected the act of being totally useless at crewing over the years that the friends had sailed together. Their performance quickly became so convincing that the men said they were more hindrance than help and it would be better if the job was left solely to them. This was, of course, exactly what the girls had hoped for. Gina and Stella claimed their favourite nooks on the foredeck, stripped down to their bikinis and started to apply sunscreen.

Lily arranged herself on her towel and lay back. She was relishing the whole experience: the breeze flowing over the deck and ruffling her hair, the warm sun caressing her body. The gentle murmur of the girls' conversation began to lull her into a daydream and she let her thoughts drift away. Ananda Giri's talk that morning had hit a chord; she had felt so separated from other people in her life, especially since her father had died. She had tried to strengthen the bond with her mother time and time again, but her mother seemed to prefer to find consolation in her grief. Lily had always thought she was the only one who felt cut off, different. It had been comforting to realise that everyone experienced that sense of separation; somehow, it made her feel less isolated. The movement of the boat lulled Lily into a gentle doze and, letting go of her thoughts, she slipped from wakefulness.

"Lily! Wake up!" A shadow fell over her body and she opened one sleepy eye to see Stella blocking the sun's rays.

"Stella! You're going to spoil my tan," she murmured.

"Never mind that! We're going snorkelling before we have lunch. Don't forget, we have to be at our afternoon session for three o'clock."

Lily yawned and rolled over, "I think I'll just stay here, I'm so comfortable."

"Scott! Lily needs some help waking up," called Stella. "Nothing like an invigorating dip for that."

Lily could hear his footsteps coming towards them; she felt slightly anxious but she was sure they wouldn't actually do what they were proposing. She decided to call their bluff.

"You wouldn't dare," she said confidently, without opening her eyes. Without any further warning, Scott scooped her up and walked to the back of the boat where he dangled her over the side.

"Put me down!" she squealed, squirming in vain. Scott was clearly enjoying her predicament, laughing so much he was in danger of dropping her. Lily looked up at his handsome face, so close to her own, seeing every detail: his light blue eyes crinkling with laughter, the small scar at the side of his mouth, his very white but not quite perfect teeth. She gave a sudden forceful wriggle and splashed into the ocean. As the cold water closed over her she let its embrace calm her tingling body; curling into a ball, she sank for a few moments before she allowed her natural buoyancy to bring her to the surface. When Scott had picked her up she had felt the same *frisson* as the previous evening, only now it was magnified a hundredfold. She'd wriggled from his arms before the electricity in her body had propelled her into the water of its own accord. She hoped Scott hadn't sensed her reaction. She had really thought the chemistry she had felt last night had been the result of heightened emotions, but now she had to face the fact that she was hugely attracted to him. She couldn't believe this had happened. The last thing she had wanted from this week was to fall for a man – especially one whose girlfriend was with him. And at a seminar on spirituality! It really couldn't be more of a disaster. She would have to get through the next couple of hours and then she would keep out of his way for the rest of the week.

She broke the surface a little way from the boat and saw her friends lined up at the stern with anxious expressions on their faces.

"Are you OK?" asked Stella with obvious concern. "We were beginning to think you'd swallowed some water when you went in. Scott was just about to dive in after you."

"You keep away from me," Lily called from the water, glaring at Scott. "It's quite clear that you can't be trusted around water."

"I'm real sorry," Scott was smiling again now that he could see Lily was all right. "I wasn't actually going to throw you in, but you just wriggled a bit too hard."

"Well, now I'm in I might as well stay here," said Lily treading water. "Stella, are you coming in? Can you bring me a mask and snorkel?"

Tom, Stella and Scott joined her in the water; Gina had decided to stay on board saying her pregnant belly made her far too buoyant in the water.

"It makes the hydrodynamics all wrong and I have to work extra hard to swim," she said, leaning on the rail. "You guys have fun. I'll have lunch ready for you when you come back."

They swam a little way from the boat and were soon above a beautiful reef. Schools of brightly-coloured fish flitted about like glittering gemstones, turning in unison and darting away from the intruders; a perfect example of Rajesh's illustration of how nature operates instinctively by collective consciousness. The water was so clear that it felt as if the reef was only a few feet away but, when they came to the surface, Stella assured Lily that it was actually about twenty feet below them.

"When we go under again, look over to the left where the ledge drops away," she said. "If you look carefully, you can see the remains of an old schooner that sailed too close to the reef. There are lots of wrecks like that in these waters. Pity we don't have more time, we could have hired a dive-master for the day and really explored. Never mind. Next time."

The men were being more adventurous, swimming close to the reef before coming up for air. Lily wasn't as experienced at breathing through the snorkel; she kept getting her mouth full of water and decided to go back and help Gina with lunch. The real reason for heading back to the boat was that she couldn't help herself from stealing glances at Scott's athletic body as he thrust himself powerfully through the water. It was doing nothing to keep her libido under control; she felt as though she was sitting in a room full of chocolate biscuits on the first day of a diet. Much better to take herself out of temptation's way.

Lily took a leisurely swim back to the boat and clambered aboard. She dried herself quickly, wrapping her hair up in a towel and went to help Gina lay out the lunch that the resort had provided for them. She found the redhead in the galley, with tears running down her face.

"Gina! What's wrong?" asked Lily, hurrying over to put her arm around the crying woman's shoulders.

"Oh, don't worry about me, Honey," she replied with a watery grin. "It's my hormones, they're ambushing me quite regularly at the moment."

"Is there anything I can do?"

"No, nothing," Gina reassured her, drying her eyes on a piece of kitchen towel. "When I feel like this I throw myself into cooking. It's amazing that Tom doesn't weigh twenty stone, with the amount of baking I've been doing lately. He likes the baking but the tears are another matter."

"But he must have seen all of this before, this is your fifth baby, isn't it?" asked Lily, looking perplexed.

"Yes, it is, but all my pregnancies went really smoothly before," explained Gina. "Tom is a wonderful man but there is only so much random crying he can cope with. It frustrates him when he can't solve a problem. He equates crying with me being unhappy and reasons that if he can find the source of my unhappiness, he can fix it. Unfortunately, that formula doesn't work with hormones that make you cry just because you've seen a squashed butterfly or a beautiful flower. It's all too abstract for Tom to deal with."

"That's not very understanding of him," said Lily.

"He's really tried and is usually very supportive. It just makes him feel helpless, which is something he just isn't used to," said Gina, rising to her husband's defence. "And like I said, all of my other pregnancies were a breeze, so this has been a bit of a surprise for both of us. Mind you, the blessing we had yesterday really seemed to help," she added thoughtfully, "I had my best night's sleep for weeks."

"Maybe that will continue."

"Let's hope so," replied Gina, fervently. "Anyway, enough about me. How was your swim?"

"The water's lovely and the reef is so beautiful, even from a distance," Lily replied, enthusiastically. "It's like an underwater jungle."

"Better than an aquarium, isn't it? There are even sea horses living there, which is quite unusual these days. I can't wait until the children are old enough to dive with us."

"I saw quite a bit of it but I'm not very good at snorkelling, so I thought I'd come back and help with lunch before I swallowed half the ocean."

"What a shame!" exclaimed Gina. "Scott's really good at teaching snorkelling. He helped me master it when Tom's attempts were coming close to drowning me. He would have helped you if you'd asked."

Lily nodded in reply, busying herself with putting the cutlery on the table. Gina observed her quietly, noting how quiet Lily had become at the mention of Scott's name. She'd also noticed how Scott had been looking at Lily as she sunbathed. She had known him a long time, so it had been very easy to deduce that he liked this elegant, feminine woman, though she didn't think he was aware of it himself yet.

She sighed. Part of her wanted to tell Lily that Marcie and Scott had split up last night but she wasn't the type of person who liked to meddle in other people's affairs. Anyway, Scott had asked them to keep the news to themselves. Marcie had talked about leaving on the morning flight but he had persuaded her to stay and finish the seminar, promising that he wouldn't tell anyone about the split apart from Gina and Tom, in case she needed someone to talk to. Stella didn't even know. Lily's eyes had held a fleeting look of such sadness that it had made her heart ache. Gina wanted to let her know that she didn't need to reproach herself for being attracted to Scott; he was, after all, one of the most decent, funny, attractive men she knew. She had only known Lily a few days but already sensed that she might be very good for Scott. There was a sensitivity and consideration about her that Gina found really appealing. Marcie was a really great girl but she was very focused on her career and her goals. Lily was obviously a people person, and that, thought Gina, was what Scott needed.

They were just putting the last dishes on the table when they heard the others climbing back on to the boat.

"I'm starving!" Tom was the first to appear below deck. "You are an angel, having everything ready for us," he said, kissing his wife hello. Scott and Stella joined them, laughing about a comical-looking pelican that had just flown over. They all sat down and began to devour the meal.

"Nothing like a good swim to sharpen the appetite," said Scott cheerfully, helping himself to a generous plate of food. "Did you see that amazing school of angel fish, Tom? They passed the reef just above the clump of blue coral."

"I did," mumbled Tom, his mouth full. "Magnificent!"

"I saw a baby octopus," added Stella. "I'd forgotten how fast those things can move if you disturb them."

"Pity I didn't see it," added Scott. "I love fresh octopus. It would have made a nice addition to lunch."

Gina shook her head. "I was never very good at admiring something in all its living vibrancy one minute and eating it the next. You'd have been on your own preparing that dish."

Lily had tucked herself away at the far end of the table, as far as she could be from Scott. She joined in the conversation from time to time but was quieter than the rest of the rowdy bunch. Gina thought she might have to do a little interfering after all.

Lunch had been demolished, leaving the friends with that drowsy, replete feeling that comes after vigorous exercise and good food.

"I'd love a siesta. It would be great if we had the afternoon free," said Tom, "but we have to start heading back in an hour or so. Leave that, Honey," he said to his wife, who had started to clear the table. "You go and relax, I'll finish up here."

"I'll help," said Stella, getting to her feet. She waved away Lily's offer to lend a hand. "There isn't enough space in here for all of us. Go and enjoy some sun."

The three of them climbed back on to the deck and into the glorious early afternoon. The sky was azure-blue and cloudless, a gentle breeze rippling the sails. It was the kind of day you'd order from a catalogue if you could. .

"Would you put some lotion on my back?" asked Gina, waving her bottle of sunscreen at Lily. "With my colouring I have to be careful. It's Factor 30, so I end up feeling as greasy as a French fry and don't change colour at all. Oh well. It's got to be done."

Lily sat behind the redhead, applying the lotion to her back.

Scott sat down next to her.

"Do you want me to do your back at the same time?" he asked.

"Ummm, no, it's all right," said Lily thinking it was the thing she wanted least and most in the world at that particular moment. "Gina can do me in a minute."

"OK," he said cheerfully, wandering off to see if he could spot any dolphins from the stern of the boat.

"There. All done," said Lily, holding out the bottle of lotion.

"Thanks. Turn around and I'll return the favour. You know, you shouldn't feel bad about liking Scott," she said kindly, rubbing in the sunscreen. "Oh, sorry, Honey, I didn't mean to be tactless," she said in response to the horrified look Lily gave her over her shoulder. "Nobody else knows," she added quickly.

"How did you guess?" asked Lily miserably, turning around to sit beside Gina.

"Oh, it's nothing anyone else would have picked up," she said, "but I was right next to you when Scott was horsing around, pretending he was going to throw you in. You were eye-to-eye and, just for a moment, you looked totally vulnerable, then you twisted out of his arms and dropped into the water." She patted Lily's hand consolingly. "We can't choose who we like and when we like them. Everyone wants to find a special person to share their life with; it's only natural and normal. You mustn't beat yourself up for how you feel; it's just a sign that you're ready to open up your heart again."

"But it's so inappropriate," said Lily woefully, rubbing her hand across her face. "He's got a girlfriend and we're here on a seminar about Oneness; I don't think the guides would be very impressed by any relationship-wrecking that went on."

"That's just the interpretation you're putting on the situation," replied Gina firmly. "Are you intending to wreck Scott's relationship? No, I thought not," she responded to Lily's shaking head. "And what I've seen of the guides, they are the least judgemental people

I've come across. All I'm saying, Honey, is that you deserve to be happy. Be prepared to open up and allow yourself to receive the beautiful gifts life has for you."

Tom stuck his head though the galley's hatch. "Scott! We should start getting the boat ready to sail back."

"OK, man, I'm with you," called Scott, leaving his look-out to start unfurling the mainsail.

Lily took Gina's hand. "Thanks, you've been really kind this afternoon."

"Don't mention it," replied Gina, patting Lily's cheek. "The universe moves in mysterious ways. Expecting the unexpected keeps you open to all its possibilities." She turned her attention to her husband.

"Home, James!" she shouted, with a cheeky grin.

Tom tugged his forelock, "Anything you say, m'lady."

Chapter 10

"What's going on?" grumbled Rod. "Why are we all sitting out here?"

"The guides decided to see us all individually, to see if we have anything we'd particularly like to discuss," offered Tom.

"Why didn't anyone tell me? I could have had another round of golf," retorted Rod in exasperation.

"If you'd been here on time," said Daphne, looking pointedly at her watch, "Rajesh would have told you himself. Private sessions have been arranged because those of our number who are less evolved," she looked at him pointedly, "have apparently had some issues with the concept of the blessing. Of course, we must understand that not everyone can be so in tune with spiritual matters," she finished smugly.

"Well, I'm not wasting my time hanging around here," Rod scowled, stomping off.

"Your loss!" called Daphne after him. "Poor man," she said to the rest of the group. "He's a long way from receiving any spiritual insights. We must pity him."

Lily was looking at the woman with an expression of absolute disbelief. Seeing that Lily was about to say something, Stella nudged her with her foot. Lily looked up, catching her friend's eye.

"Don't take her so seriously," Stella whispered, a smile crinkling her eyes.

"I can't believe that woman is so self-satisfied!" Lily whispered back. "Who on earth would ever go to her for any kind of coaching? You'd be more messed-up than ever after she'd got her hands on you."

Scott had just finished his session and returned to the reception. "Lily, Rajesh would like to see you now," he said, looking slightly distracted.

Lily walked across the lounge to the far end where the guide was sitting waiting for her. She felt slightly nervous at the thought of having his undivided attention; it reminded her of talking to Mrs Stephens, her favourite English teacher, who had encouraged Lily to make a career of her writing. Next to Lily's father, Mrs Stephens was the kindest, most encouraging influence in her life during her late teens, but she could always see straight through Lilyh and wouldn't countenance anything less than her best efforts. She could picture her clearly, even after all these years, her silver hair swept into a French plait in what Lily thought was the epitome of bohemian chic. Her ankle-length skirts swished as she walked, accompanied by the percussion of her bangles.

"You are a gifted writer," she used to say, fixing Lily with her striking blue gaze, "and you owe it to yourself to add your best efforts to that talent. Few people have the gift of communication; you are able to make words come alive with subtlety and humour. Make sure you choose each word you write as though you are picking the finest ingredients for a gastronomic feast. There is enough literary junk food out there, please do not add to it."

Lily wasn't convinced that she'd reached the literary heights that Mrs Stephens had aspired for her, but her teaching had inspired her to always produce the best piece of work possible. That being said, the novel wasn't going too well. She felt as though something was blocking her which was unusual for Lily. Her journalistic training had been a good foil against getting caught up in the vagaries of creative writing. She was disciplined in her approach and didn't usually experience writer's block. Oh well, she thought, there was a first time for everything. Perhaps Rajesh could shed some light on the situation.

The guide smiled and gestured that she sit down in the seat opposite him. She sat, looking expectantly at Rajesh who looked back calmly. Lily thought she had never come across anyone who was more collected than the guides. She'd watched them moving around the resort over the last couple of days, surrounded by an extraordinary air of tranquillity. It reminded her of an elderly Buddhist monk she had seen in Thailand; he had been sitting in the square outside a temple, just watching the world go by, with an expression of blissful calm on his face. He seemed to be completely in tune with life. It would be wonderful to be able to enjoy the moment like that. Lily knew her head was constantly distracted, darting about from the past to the future; usually all the attention the present received was a passing wave and the promise to pay a longer visit next time. She would like to be able to get off the hamster wheel so that she could be free from her mental chatter for a few minutes.

Rajesh was watching her as though he had all the time in the world; Lily would have liked to have enjoyed the silence with him for a few moments longer, but her conditioning kicked in and she started to worry about keeping the others waiting. She cleared her throat.

"Umm. I'm writing a book at the moment and I'm struggling a bit with writer's block, which doesn't usually happen to me. I wondered if you could throw some light on the subject."

"Often blockages in our emotions are reflected by blockages in our day-to-day experience. Is there a relationship in your life where you are experiencing an emotional blockage?" asked the guide, his voice gentle and melodious. The face of Lily's mother loomed in her mind's eye, causing her to raise her eyebrows in surprise.

"What do you see?" asked Rajesh.

"Well, my mother," said Lily, still feeling a little perplexed. "I know that we're not particularly close but I wouldn't have thought it was affecting the rest of my life."

"The relationship we have with our parents has a powerful effect on us. I can see that there is a great deal of pain in your association with her. You need to feel that pain and forgive her for not being what you needed her to be. As you forgive her and accept her just as she is, she will be able to accept you just as you are. Gradually, the relationship will be healed."

As Rajesh spoke, a myriad of images passed through Lily's mind: proudly bringing home her paintings from school to be told that they were cluttering up the place and, in future, she should leave them in her classroom; her mother constantly taking her brother's side in any dispute; being told that she had probably got bored of Matt and that's why the marriage had failed, she could never stick at anything. Re-living these memories was as harrowing as experiencing them for the first time. Lily felt that she would choke on the grief that had flooded every part of her being. Her eyes swimming with tears, she looked up to see her pain reflected in the face of the guide, it was as though he felt her every emotion.

"Give me your hands," he said. "I am going to give you a blessing."

As Rajesh held Lily's hands, she felt the blessing envelop her like a cashmere blanket. Her pain, so intense only moments earlier, began to dissolve like mist in the warmth of the sun. She sat, with her eyes closed, allowing the experience to have its full effect and, little by little, the pain ebbed away. She had no idea that those small incidences had made such an impact, that gradually, over forty years, they had caused her to shut herself away, building a wall to protect her from being hurt. It was only when she had seen the pain in Rajesh's eyes that she felt truly understood for the first time in her life and, feeling understood, she had been able to let that pain go.

"The Divine does not wish you to be trapped in your suffering; just put your attention on it, acknowledge it instead of running from it, and the charges attached to it will dissipate," Rajesh was speaking gently. Lily opened her eyes to focus on what he was saying. "Take some time now to be alone and let the process continue. It will bring greater insights as the experience deepens."

Lily thanked the guide and made her way out to reception where the remainder of the group was gathered.

"You look a bit bowled over," said Stella, standing up to give her a hug. "I'm going for my session now but we'll catch up later. Go and have a lie-down."

Lily nodded her thanks to her friend and made her way back to the bure. Sitting on the edge of her bed, she slipped off her shoes and outer clothes and slid under the sheets. What a strange experience, to see all those episodes from her life flit in front of her eyes. She had no idea that she had buried the pain deep inside her, not allowing herself to feel the emotions she had suppressed. Letting go of all that stale energy had left her feeling much lighter but physically drained. She closed her eyes and allowed herself to drift, soon falling into a deep, peaceful sleep.

She dreamed that she was watching herself as a little girl, playing with her brother. They were becoming quite boisterous, fighting over a book but with no malice towards each other. Lily saw herself snatch the hardback away from her brother and run squealing around the couch, holding the treasured item as high in the air as she could, out of his grasp. He was pursuing her doggedly but was too small to have any hope of winning back The Tale of Samuel Whiskers. Their mother was writing at her desk in the corner of the room; she had been watching the horseplay, rubbing her left temple. Suddenly she called out sharply, "Lily, stop tormenting your brother and give him back his book. You're not being fair, he's much smaller than you."

"Sorry, Mummy." Lily felt her heart go out to her six-year-old self; the little girl's expression was so dejected. As the children carried on playing quietly, Lily turned her attention to her mother and what she saw moved her even more deeply. She had her head in her hands and was trembling from her efforts to hide her tears. What had made her so upset? From her detached perspective, Lily could see that it wasn't the children's play. A sense of empathy for the unhappy woman rose within her and she wished she could go and put her arms around her mother. At the age of six she had been too young to understand that the scenario could be seen from another viewpoint but she could see it clearly now. Her pain had been created out of the meaning she had put on the experience; she hadn't been able to comprehend that her mother's upset had been nothing to do with her.

Dreaming in a bure on a tropical island, thousands of miles from home, Lily was finally able to appreciate that her mother had been struggling with challenges she was completely unaware of, and to forgive her.

Scott sat on his branch at the waterfall, mulling over his session with Rajesh. He was a little surprised about how practical the guide had been in answering his questions. He'd always found spiritual people a little too airy-fairy in his experience; often they were focused on struggling through life in the hope of receiving some sort of reward at the end of it. Rajesh had been very pragmatic when Scott had told him that he and Marcie had split up and had not tried to persuade him to forge reconciliation.

"Now you will both be able to follow your individual paths and live more fulfilled lives. You must not be regretful when a relationship comes to the end of its time. Be grateful for the time you have spent together and the lessons you have learned. Do all that you can to make the separation as painless as possible for each of you, always remembering that you have brought much love and joy into each other's lives in the past."

Scott had been a little taken aback by the guide's forthright advice and was still contemplating it when the guide asked him a question.

"What do you really want to do with your life, Scott?"

"That's a question that I have been asking myself for months but it isn't exactly easy to answer."

Rajesh regarded him unwaveringly. "It would be easy to answer if you let go of other people's expectations and asked yourself what you truly want. If you have no compelling purpose for your life, you will feel as though you are constantly drifting; if you have a purpose and do not act on it, your life will feel stagnant. I will give you a blessing with the intention that what you really desire will become clear to you."

The guide had placed his hands on Scott's head and Scott had felt the now familiar sensation of peace and calm descending upon him. He had thanked Rajesh who advised him to spend some time alone that afternoon in reflection. He decided that he would go back to his bure first, to make sure that Marcie was OK. She was the first person to have a private session this afternoon and he hadn't seen her since.

Marcie was asleep in the hammock on their veranda but woke when she heard Scott's footfall on the wooden deck and opened one sleepy eye.

"I'm sorry I disturbed you," said Scott, crouching next to the hammock and taking her hand. "How are you doing?"

"Not bad," she said, opening the other eye and blinking at him. "What time is it?"

"Five-thirty."

"Five-thirty! I've been asleep for two hours!"

"Well, you obviously needed it," he smiled. "You're looking much better." He was relieved to see that her eyes were no longer red from crying and that she seemed calm for the first time in the last few days.

She nodded. "I am much better. The talk with Rajesh really helped," she paused, reflecting on the session. "He wasn't at all surprised that we had split up."

"I know. Did he say anything about it?"

"Only that we be kind and respectful to each other. He told me not to see the ending as a failure but part of my journey. Then he told me that I had been wrong thinking that I'd never been able to please my father. He said Dad had always been so proud of me but he couldn't tell me how he felt because of the way he'd been brought up. Not being able to show any emotion, you know?"

"How did you feel about that?" asked Scott, gently.

"I bawled my eyes out," she replied, sitting up. "That's when I realised just how spiritual those guys are. I've never seen a man so undisturbed by a woman crying. He just sat there quietly, letting me cry, without making me feel embarrassed or trying to make me stop."

Scott laughed, glad to see she was regaining her sense of irony. "No, there aren't many men who would be so composed in the face of a sobbing woman." He continued thoughtfully, "So, did what he say make sense to you?"

"Completely. I realised I'd spent my whole life trying to please someone who was already as pleased as he could be with me. I can't wait to get home and talk to Dad about it, to tell him how much his love and support means to me." She smiled in anticipation, looking more relaxed than Scott had seen her for a long time.

"I'm glad Rajesh helped you. Those guys must be mind-readers. They seem to know just what's going on with everyone," said Scott, looking bemused. "He told me that I needed to find a compelling purpose for my life or I would never feel fulfilled. I know! I know!" he said, holding up his hand as Marcie started to speak. "It's what you've been telling me for ages."

Marcie laughed. "Yes, but it's easier to hear from Rajesh because he doesn't have an agenda," she said honestly. "Well, it sounds as though we both got what we needed from our meetings with him. I'd be curious to know whether everyone else has the same sort of experience."

"It would be interesting to be a fly on the wall during Rod's session," said Scott, grinning widely.

"He'd be a hard nut to crack, all right," she replied, smiling. "Scottie," she continued, pushing his hair back off his forehead, "I'm glad we're going through this here. If it had happened anywhere else, I think I would have found it too hard to be reasonable and I'd really hate to lose your friendship."

He enveloped her in a bear-hug, speaking softly into her ear, "Me, too. We'll always be friends."

He watched a fish flip over in the pool, its tail breaking the surface of the water. What was it he'd really like to do if he was only pleasing himself? The answer came as soon as he had asked the question and it was so obvious, it made him laugh out loud. He wanted to mentor teenagers from poor backgrounds, coaching them in sports and helping them to get past the low expectations of their upbringing. Yes! That was what he really wanted to do! He'd speak to his father as soon as he was back in New York. Whistling, Scott swung himself down from the tree and started to make his way back down to the resort for the evening meeting.

Chapter 11

At 6:45 p.m. Rajesh's group met at the reception lounge. They were to have their first blessing experience with what had been described as Oneness Beings, a term that Lily found a little disconcerting. She was discussing the matter with Stella while they waited for the guide to arrive; Stella hadn't met these Beings either and they were trying to imagine what to expect.

"I hope they don't pull back a screen and ET's sitting there," said Lily. "That would really freak me out."

"Or Gizmo, from Gremlins," giggled Stella. "You'd have to be careful not to let him have anything to eat. It wouldn't really be conducive to having an experience of Oneness."

"Really, girls!" Daphne's patronising voice cut across the conversation. "I thought you two would be more aware. The Oneness Beings are people who have chosen to dedicate themselves to a life of meditation. They deserve to be treated with respect."

Daphne's disparaging comments only made the girls giggle even more. The older woman was about to deliver another rebuke when the guide arrived, causing a welcome distraction.

"Are we ready?" he beamed. "Let us proceed to the main bure for the blessing."

"Rajesh, could you explain a little more about what we can expect?" asked Tom. "You know that this experience is new to most of us here and we'd be grateful if you'd explain what is going to happen."

"Of course, Tom," the guide replied respectfully. "The Oneness Beings are men and women who have dedicated themselves to a life of meditation." Out of the corner of her eye, Lily could see Daphne puffing out her chest at Rajesh's description. "Because they meditate almost constantly," he continued, "they have reached a very divine state of consciousness. When they give a person the blessing, some of their awareness and insights are transferred, allowing the person to have a greater experience of Oneness."

"And that's all?" asked John cautiously, "I don't want to find myself suddenly wearing a kaftan and chanting all day."

"Why do you think that The Divine wishes to impose anything on you?" asked Rajesh, seriously. "The experience of the blessing causes a change that allows you to be free of biological and social conditioning. As the experience deepens, it causes you to be truly atease with yourself as you are, without constantly struggling and striving to be someone else. This is your natural state. The Divine does not wish you to become someone that you are not. We are all different, like the many facets of a finely-cut diamond."

"Well, I think I could handle that," said John, sounding reassured.

Following the guide to the main bure, Lily noticed that Scott and Marcie seemed to have resolved their differences. He had his arm around her shoulders as they walked and she was looking calm, though a little subdued. Lily was genuinely glad for them and tried to brush away the pang she felt for herself. It was silly to have even entertained the thought that there was any chance of something developing between herself and Scott; Scott was from a different world and they didn't even live on the same continent. She laughed to herself. Ever the romantic! She was glad that she could focus her attention on the guides' teachings now and stop distracting herself by daydreaming about Scott.

They reached the meeting hall and entered quietly. Today it was lit entirely by candles that flickered gently in the draught as the door opened. A haunting piece of music was playing in the background, its melodious lyrics being sung in a language that Lily didn't understand but found deeply soothing. Some of the other groups had already arrived and were meditating quietly or gazing at the two figures seated on the platform at the front of the room. Both men were dressed in white and were sitting with their eyes closed in deep meditation. One of them was light-skinned and the other dark, like the guides. Lily wasn't sure that she would have called them angelic, but they definitely had a quality of other-worldliness about them. She found them fascinating. Lily noticed Rod, sitting in the row in front watching them, the expression on his face a cross between curiosity and trepidation. It was the first time she had seen him let his guard down. She exhaled deeply, realising that, like herself, most people constantly wore the masks of the identities they had created for themselves, too scared to see themselves, or other people, as they really were. He caught sight of her watching him and, straight away, his mask was back in place.

"They look as if they've been let out of the funny farm," he growled. "Oneness Beings, my arse." Lily's feelings of empathy dissolved instantaneously. Horrible, vulgar man! He'd completely spoiled the moment. How could she possibly receive a blessing when she was in such an angry state?

She sat there fuming for a few moments, as the guides began to gesture to individuals to go up and receive their blessings from the two mesmerising figures, then she gradually let go of her anger as she became absorbed by the process. A small queue had formed to the left-hand side of the stage and, at the guides' signal, the next person would go and stand in front of the first man who would place his hands on their head, just as the guides had done. After maybe a minute, the person would move on to receive the second blessing, before being directed to sit on one of the bean-bags in the centre of the room and soak up the experience.

The two Oneness Beings wore expressions of pure bliss as they placed their hands on each person's head. It was as though they were the personification of joy. Every so often, the fair-skinned man would erupt into laughter as he placed his hands on someone's head, as though it delighted him to be able to give the blessing. Part of Lily found the whole experience surreal, yet, at the same time, it felt completely natural. She felt a sense of quiet expectation and made up her mind to be open to whatever this evening's unusual experience would bring. When Rajesh signalled to her a few minutes later, she walked calmly to the front of the room and joined the queue.

When it was her turn, the first man placed his hands on her head and she experienced the familiar sense of well-being as before. As she moved over to the second Oneness Being, he placed his hands on her head and began to laugh. To her surprise, she began to laugh, too. At first, she fought the urge, thinking it might be disrespectful, butthe laughter continued to bubble up and she couldn't hold on to it any longer.

"Ha, ha, ha, ha!" she chortled. "Oh! Hee, hee, hee, hee, hee!" Lily felt like an exuberant child. She didn't even know what she was laughing at but she didn't care; the feeling was too good to suppress. She was still giggling as a guide led her back to one of the bean-bags, where she lay back and closed her eyes, intending to enjoy every moment of this heady feeling.

She wasn't sure how long she lay there, enjoying her bliss. From time to time, she was aware of other people dissolving into laughter, some snuffling quietly and some erupting into loud gaffaws; the atmosphere in the hall was one of jubilation. Eventually, Lily opened her eyes and sat up, catching Rajesh's eye, who indicated that it was time to leave. She rose slowly to her feet, still feeling the residue of the laughter rising from her belly, and made her way carefully through her supine companions towards the door. Outside, she found that she was the last of her group to leave; the others were gathered together to one side, waiting for the guide's instructions for tomorrow. Rajesh, following closely behind Lily, joined the group and explained what would be happening the next day.

"Dinner is being served in the restaurant. Go and eat, savouring not only the food but also the experiences you have enjoyed this evening. We will meet with the others tomorrow morning at eight-thirty to hear Ananda Giri's teachings and, in the afternoon, you will meet with me again at three o'clock."

"Rajesh, before you go can I ask you something?" said Lily. "Why were some of us laughing this evening?"

"Do you think that The Divine does not enjoy laughter?" asked the guide. "Who do you think created humour? For too long we have considered spirituality to be serious and dry, a duty that was to be fulfilled in the hope of some distant reward. No, true spirituality is a sense of being connected to everything; this brings joy which is expressed in laughter," he smiled. "Everyone's experience is different; if you did not laugh, it does not mean that your experience is any less powerful. Go and eat now. We will discuss these things more fully tomorrow."

The guide slipped quietly back into the hall to continue overseeing the process and the small group made its way to the restaurant. Everyone else was still in the hall as Rajesh's group had been given their blessings first, so they chose the largest table available and sat down together to share their thoughts. Lily was still grinning like a Cheshire cat, though the gales of laughter seemed to have finally passed. John was eying her curiously and eventually spoke.

"So what did it feel like?"

"The laughter?" Lily beamed. "It was such a surprise! I wasn't feeling particularly in tune with what was going on; I didn't think I was even in the right frame of mind to receive a blessing. When the second man put his hands on my head, I don't know what happened but I just felt such a sense of joy, like Rajesh said, and I couldn't stop laughing."

"You look as if you've lost ten years," said Gina, enviously. "If they could bottle that, they'd make a fortune."

"I feel great," agreed Lily enthusiastically. "It was an extraordinary sensation." She caught Marcie's eye across the table and smiled warmly.

"How about you, Marcie?" she asked. "What was it like for you this evening?"

"Oh, I don't know …" the young woman began cautiously. "It's the same feeling as when I've had a couple of glasses of really good wine. You know, the quality kind that isn't going to give you a hangover. I know it's maybe not the most appropriate analogy," she continued, seeing Daphne purse her lips disapprovingly, "but you know what I mean."

"Like a good Pinot Noir?" asked Lily.

"Exactly right!" said Marcie, smiling back.

"Well, we all look like we've had a really good night's sleep," said Stella. "Even you, Rod," she added, trying to provoke him. She needn't have wasted her energy; the Texan just grunted and continued, head down, to demolish an unreasonably large plate of food. Lily and Stella exchanged a conspiratorial look, quickly breaking eye-contact to prevent them from bursting into laughter.

The group continued their meal and the conversation moved on to discussing how they had spent their free time that morning.

"Brenda and I went down to the far end of the beach and just cuddled up in one of those hammocks," said John. "Felt like we were teenagers again."

Brenda smiled pinkly. "It's so nice to be able to take time for just the two of us. Can't remember the last time we did that."

"What have you been up to, Daphne?" asked Stella.

"I'm going to be very busy with my clients when I get home," she replied importantly. "I've been looking through some case studies."

"You should just relax and unwind," added Scott. "Who knows when you'll have the opportunity to enjoy such an idyllic experience again?"

"Who, indeed?" she replied, busying herself with her meal.

Stella caught Lily's eye again and raised an eyebrow. It was unusual for Daphne to be so subdued. Perhaps something was bothering the woman. She decided to ask her.

"Is everything all right, Daphne?"

"Of course," she snapped, "why shouldn't it be?"

"It's just that you seem a little quiet," replied Stella, wishing she'd never started the conversation.

Daphne began to speak through clenched teeth, her face flushing an unattractive shade of puce.

"If you must know, I'm sick and tired of all of you! This is a spiritual retreat and all you do is laugh and joke about like a bunch of children. None of you are taking it seriously."

"But Rajesh just said that we're not supposed to be serious," offered Gina tentatively.

"Ooohhh! That's exactly what I mean!" retorted Daphne, getting up from the table and flouncing out of the restaurant, leaving the group gaping after her in surprise.

"What do you think has got into Daphne?" Gina asked the others at the table.

"Needs to get laid," replied Rod, not looking up from his food

Chapter 12

Nelson had dropped Lily at the local village so that she could buy some souvenirs to take back to England with her. She wandered from stall to stall in the quaint village market, admiring the pretty hand-made jewellery and savouring the aroma of local spices that filled the air. She had bought her mother a pendant made of mother-of-pearl and was looking for a small gift for Diana; the two of them always exchanged small presents from their holidays. As she meandered along the aisles, she pondered on Ananda Giri's message from that morning. He had echoed what Rajesh had said last night, after they had received the evening blessing.

"The very act of living is joy," he had pronounced, seated crossed-legged on his chair on the platform. "True spirituality is enjoying life; anyone who is against this is against spirituality and is bad for society. A joyful man is kind, considerate and generous, he cares about his fellow man and is good for society."

His message was so simple on one hand and so challenging on the other. He had gone on to say that, as people truly accepted themselves as they were, embracing all the aspects of their personalities including those parts that society had deemed as unacceptable – such as fear, anger, jealousy and weakness – then they would be truly at peace with themselves.

"As you deny these parts of yourself and run from them they fight for survival, becoming stronger and stronger even as you try to subdue them. Instead, as you acknowledge them in the moment, experiencing each emotion fully as it arises, the negative charge is dispelled instead of building to a point where it explodes."

Lily thought of Daphne storming out of the restaurant last night; something had clearly being building in her for a while to cause such a reaction. She could recognise the same reaction when she tried to deny part of herself. As soon as she decided she had been over-indulging in chocolate and made the decision to cut it out of her diet completely for a while, she was seized with obsession and could think of nothing else but eating it. She'd never really thought that suppressing emotions and desires caused them to become stronger but, in the light of Ananda Giri's teachings, it seemed to make sense.

She came across a stall of vibrant clothing and picked up a scarf of entwined ribbons of emerald and turquoise on a black background; it would be perfect for Diana. Smiling, she paid the shy village lady and continued her meandering, still deep in reflection.

Of course, society didn't help people to accept themselves as they were. The media constantly displayed images of twig-thin girls as being the desired expression of female beauty and no man could expect to win the girl of his dreams unless he was driving around in the latest flashy car. Her lips formed a moue. On one level, everyone knew that it was just advertising but it was insidious; given long enough, those images formed an unconscious blueprint, dictating what was acceptable and what missed the mark. In everything she wrote she tried to dispel the illusion that sucked in so many teenage girls: that they were too fat or not pretty enough when compared to the models in glossy magazines. She constantly reassured them that they were lovely exactly as they were, with all the individual quirkiness that might have disqualified them from being conventional beauties.

Lily realised that she had spent too much of her life conforming to other people's ideas of how she should live and it had only caused her to feel as though she was constantly changing masks, adapting to whoever she was with at the time. It was exhausting and, at times, she had no idea of who she really was or what she wanted from life. The guides' message was giving her hope that she might be absolutely fine just as she was. She was starting to feel she might have the courage to be herself and let the masks drop.

The midday sun was hot on her neck. Lily looked at her watch: 11:45 a.m. Nelson wasn't coming to pick her up for another three-quarters of an hour. She was feeling thirsty and wanted to find some shade to shield her from the heat of the day. Nelson had told her there was a sort of café bar at the far end of the market and she began to move more purposefully, heading towards the cluster of tables she glimpsed beyond the last stalls.

She was nearly there when she noticed Scott sitting under the cool canopy of branches that shaded the café. He was reading a newspaper as he drank his coffee and hadn't looked up. Hopefully she had time to retrace her steps without him noticing her; she didn't want to end up in another private encounter. Despite having sensed a tentative connection with Marcie last night, she still felt drawn to Scott. She had been aware of his every word and gesture at the dinner table. There was a good example of suppressed desire intensifying, she thought ruefully.

She was walking quickly back towards the market stalls when she heard him call her name.

"Lily! Didn't you see me? Come and have a cup of coffee."

She stopped, feeling torn between embarrassment and the need to get away from him.

Turning, she gave him a wave.

"Oh, hi Scott! I've just realised the time. I don't want to keep Nelson waiting." Lily began to walk away again but heard the sound of running footsteps behind her.

"Hey! What's up?" said Scott, looking perplexed as he drew alongside her. "I spoke to Nelson earlier. He's coming to pick us both up at twelve-thirty. Why are you rushing off?"

"I need to pick up a few more bits and pieces. I remembered I haven't bought anything for my nieces yet," she laughed. "I'm turning into an English eccentric."

"Lily, is everything OK?" asked Scott, putting his hand on her arm. "You're acting a bit strange."

Feeling the familiar bolt of electricity shoot through her body at his touch, Lily snatched her arm away, stepping backwards.

"I just need a little time to myself at the moment," she said, trying to smile. "Feeling a little out of sorts, that's all."

Scott expression grew even more concerned. "I'm not letting you wander off in this heat if you're not feeling well. Come and sit down in the shade."

"Please, Scott! I'm fine! Just leave me alone!" Lily could hear the anguish in her voice and knew she had made an utter fool of herself. She hurried away, leaving him standing between the stalls looking confused and hurt. How could she have been so stupid! She should have just gone and sat down with him like a mature adult, instead of behaving like some deranged woman in a tacky amateur play. She was surprised she hadn't held her hand to her tortured brow as she exited theatrically, stage right! What a drama queen! She'd never be able to look Scott in the face again. She certainly couldn't cope with the idea of sharing the jeep with him. He was too caring to let matters rest and would want to reassure himself that she was really all right. There was nothing she could say to him about her agitated state.

The resort was only twenty minutes away on foot. Lily set off, walking as quickly as she could in her unsuitable strappy sandals, hoping she would get back before Nelson passed her on the road. She didn't feel like explaining her behaviour to anyone. The heat of the sun was intense and after about five minutes she felt the back of her neck beginning to burn. Great! She'd probably get sunstroke now, too. Nearly half an hour later, she arrived back at the resort. Thankfully, she slipped in unnoticed by Nelson, who was manoeuvring the jeep through the tall gates. Lily limped back to her bure, her feet blistered and sore, to find Stella drinking tea with Gina on the porch. She couldn't have felt less like company.

"Hello, lovely girl!" said Stella. "Managed to get your shopping, then? Let's have a look."

"Do you mind if we wait until later," Lily said tremulously. "I really need a shower. Sorry not to be more sociable, Gina. I'll catch up with you both later."

"Well! What was that all about?" Stella's strident tones followed her into the bure. "She looked really upset."

Lily's tears mingled with the water from the shower and were washed away. Her head was throbbing and she felt emotionally drained. She'd grown really fond of the two women sitting on the porch but she would have preferred they hadn't seen her distress. Stella was bound to ask her what was going on and she really, really wanted to forget the incident had ever happened.

Happily for Lily's already overwrought state, the noise of the shower drowned the sound of a third voice joining Gina's and Stella's on the porch. Scott had returned from the village with Nelson and decided to seek Stella out and make sure that Lily was all right.

"Then she looked like she was going to burst into tears and rushed off," he was saying, as he finished recounting the story. "Has she had some bad news?"

"None that I know of," replied Stella, thoughtfully. "When she comes out of the shower, we'll try to get to the bottom of it."

"Thanks," replied Scott, gathering the bags of souvenirs he had bought at the market. "I hated to see her looking so upset. I'll go and wash up before our afternoon session. See you later."

"I wouldn't probe too hard with Lily at the moment, Stell," said Gina in a low voice, watching Scott's retreating back.

"No, I won't," agreed Stella nodding her head. "So I gather we have one of those uncomfortable love triangles."

"Well…it's actually a little more, or less, complicated than that," replied Gina with a sigh. "Scott asked Tom and me not to say anything but, in light of this afternoon's little episode, it's probably better that you know. Scott and Marcie split up a couple of days ago."

"Oh … and there's no chance of a reconciliation?"

"No. They both feel it's run its course," Gina continued. "Marcie was pretty upset at first but they both know it's time to move on. Scott, being the gentlemen he is, persuaded her to stay on so that she could finish the seminar and promised not to tell anyone, except us."

"And do you think he likes Lily?" asked Stella. "I can see that she's the type of woman that would appeal to him. Feminine, intelligent."

"I'm sure he does," said Gina with certainty, "but I don't think he realises it himself yet."

"Oh dear. And poor Lily's beating herself up for feeling attracted to him because he has a girlfriend. It's all a bit of a mess, isn't it?"

"Hmmm," her friend murmured in agreement, pouring them both another cup of tea from the pot. "It's difficult to know what to do. I mean, it's a sensitive situation for all of them. Maybe we should just keep quiet and let events unfold. We seem to be in quite a magical environment this week; I think we should just leave it to whatever higher power is working here."

"Well, as you know, it's not always easy for me to keep my mouth shut but, in this case, I think you're right," said Stella. "Though I must say I shall be watching what happens with avid interest."

Scott stepped back on to the main path and was pleased to see Tom meandering along, a little way ahead.

"Hey, buddy! Wait up!" he called, breaking into a jog. Tom paused to wait for his friend, greeting Scott with a boisterous hug.

"So, what's new? How was the market? Worth a look or full of junk that I'm going to have to dissuade Gina from buying?"

"No, it's not bad," replied Scott. "They have some interesting carvings and decent hand-made jewellery. I saw Lily down there. She was acting a little weird."

"Oh? How do you mean?" asked Tom, realising his friend had something he wanted to talk about.

"Well, I was having a coffee at a little café stall when I looked up and saw her walking away; I ran after her and asked her to join me but she seemed really distressed and told me to leave her alone. I felt like I did something to upset her but I haven't a clue what it could have been."

They had reached Tom's bure and he gestured to Scott to take a seat on the porch. After they'd come back from the sailing trip, Gina had mentioned that she thought that Lily had developed feelings for Scott that she was pushing away. It seemed that her intuition had been spot on, as always. This was the kind of drama that women loved and men hated. He wished his wife was there to be able to offer Scott some advice but she wasn't; he would just have to get on with it.

"You've spent quite a lot of time in Lily's company over the last week?"

"Yes," Scott confirmed. "Why do you ask?"

"She's a decent girl. She probably thinks Marcie wouldn't like it."

"It's all been completely innocent," replied Scott, defensively.

"I'm sure it has, but it's awkward for Lily," replied Tom. "She doesn't know you've split up and, even if she did, it would probably make the situation worse. I imagine she'd really keep her distance then."

"Why?" asked Scott, looking perplexed.

"Because she wouldn't want to be pouring salt on Marcie's wounds. You're being a little slow about all this, man."

"That seems a bit extreme. I don't know why we can't be friends."

Tom sighed. Scott was ignoring everything he was saying, which was unusual for this normally receptive man. It seemed that Gina was right with her second deduction: that Scott liked Lily but was oblivious of the fact. Perhaps he should be a little more direct.

"Say, in theory, that Lily's developed a bit of a soft spot for you," Tom continued cautiously. "You can appreciate how difficult that would be for her. Maybe that's why she didn't want to be on her own with you this morning."

Scott sat pondering his friend's words. "I hadn't thought about that," he said slowly. "Do you think that's what has happened?"

"Gina seems to think so," Tom replied. "You know how she picks up on things. I wouldn't have said anything but it looked like you weren't going to leave Lily alone; I think you need to give her some space."

"I guess you're right," agreed Scott. "I don't want to make her feel uncomfortable. Shame, though. I really enjoy her company."

"Yeah, well. Maybe you'll bump into each other again at a more opportune moment," said Tom, sorry to see the disappointment on his friend's face.

"You never know," agreed Scott with a half-hearted smile.

Chapter 13

Lily was relieved, though a little surprised, that Stella didn't press her to find out about the morning's events. She seemed content that Lily said she felt much better after a shower and a lie-down and left it at that. They made their way over to the lounge a little early, allowing her to pick a spot on a bean-bag in the corner of the room where she felt inconspicuous. She knew that Scott would behave impeccably in the circumstances but she still felt nervous at the thought of their first meeting.

The rest of the group started to arrive. Rod stomped in and claimed his usual place on the couch, next to Stella. John and Brenda arrived next, holding hands. Lily was happy to see how much Brenda had come out of herself over the last few days. Occasionally she spoke up now, instead of letting John do all the talking and he was clearly pleased by his wife's new confidence. Gina and Marcie appeared next, flanked by their men who were sharing a joke and laughing like a couple of drains. Catching Lily's eye, Scott smiled at her, mouthing, "Are you OK?" She returned the smile with a nod, grateful for his kindness. Daphne paused at the entrance before sweeping regally into the lounge and depositing herself in the chair that she had claimed on day one, right in front of the guide. She'd swap seats with Rajesh if she thought she could get away with it, thought Lily mischievously, a small smile playing around her lips. She felt a slight twinge of guilt and started to berate herself for her lack of empathy when she remembered Ananda Giri had said, that morning, they were to embrace all aspects of their personalities. Time I let my naughty little girl out, she decided, her grin widening.

Rajesh arrived and took his place at the front of the room. He smiled at the group, observing each one in turn. He's never in a rush to act, thought Lily, still intrigued by his ability to be completely in the moment. As if reading her thoughts, Tom addressed the guide.

"Rajesh, why do you sit for so long in silence before you begin our sessions?" he asked.

"I do not speak until I have something to say," replied the guide. "I wait until The Divine prompts me with the right words."

"All spiritual masters do it," interrupted Daphne. "It's called channelling."

Lily's naughty little girl was cart-wheeling around in her head, pulling faces and blowing raspberries. She didn't dare look in Stella's direction or she wouldn't be able to control her giggles. Rajesh was speaking again, as though completely unaware of the interruption.

"Let us discuss further Ananda Giri's teachings from this morning," he continued. "We are made up of a number of personalities that arise from the collective consciousness. Some of these personalities we like, such as the good person and the generous person and some we dislike, such as the jealous person or the angry person. If any of these personalities are suppressed, they begin to fight for survival. If we would only acknowledge these personalities and let them express themselves fully, they would be satisfied and take their rightful place in our lives."

"So, you're saying that if I feel horny, I should go out and try to get laid as many times as possible," said Rod, taking an interest in the session for the first time.

"No," replied Rajesh, without any trace of embarrassment. "This very lustful state occurs in people when they deny their sexuality. These suppressed feelings grow until all the person can think about is sex. If he were to acknowledge that lustfulness is part of his personality, instead of trying to subdue it, the desire would not build until it was out of control."

"So, are you saying that you have lustful thoughts?" Rod asked the guide.

"Don't be so disrespectful!" squawked Daphne, looking outraged at the Texan.

"It's all right," said Rajesh, lifting his hand to silence Daphne. "Of course I have lustful thoughts," he continued, "but I just acknowledge that it is the arising of one of the many personalities; I don't get caught up in thoughts or let them control me. I just acknowledge what is there."

"This is quite a difficult concept to grasp," said Gina, looking a little perplexed. "You're saying that if we allow ourselves to accept our faults they won't control us?"

Rajesh nodded. "It is a difficult concept to grasp, because we spend our whole time qualifying our personalities as good and bad, when they are just what they are. It is impossible to have light without the comparison of dark. We do not say that light is good and darkness is bad; we just accept them for what they are. When we do the same thing with the arising personalities, we know much greater ease and happiness in our lives; anything experienced fully is joy."

"The thought of embracing all the negative parts of my personality goes completely against my upbringing," said Gina. "That's a lot of conditioning to undo."

"This is part of the work of the blessing," replied Rajesh. "It allows you to see things from the perspective of Oneness, connectedness. Much of our frustration arises from the perception that there are personalities that are unacceptable and that we will be able to rid ourselves of the ones we do not like. We cannot do this."

"Yes, that's right," said Daphne, self-importantly. "To quote Carl Jung, 'Anything you resist persists.'"

Again Rajesh continued unperturbed, despite the embarrassed shuffling that was travelling around the room. "When we become aware of the impossibility of change, then there is peace, for grace meets us and allows us to reach a sense of completeness that we could never find ourselves."

"I'm so sorry to interrupt, but I can't keep quiet any longer." Lily was surprised to hear Brenda speaking up in the group; despite her confidence increasing, she was still quite shy.

"Yes, Brenda," said Rajesh smiling encouragingly. "What is it you would like to say?"

"I, uhmm … I'm feeling very angry and you have just told us that if I express this anger, it will dissolve. Is that right?" asked Brenda, her voice trembling with emotion.

"Yes, that is correct," affirmed the guide. "What is the cause of your anger?"

Everyone waited with rapt attention for Brenda to answer, especially John who was as surprised as anybody to hear his wife expressing herself in public.

"Oh dear," she continued, "I'm so embarrassed. It's just that Daphne has interrupted every session. Sorry," she whispered in the older woman's direction, without looking up. "And I have been brought up to believe it's polite to sit quietly when someone is speaking, so that everyone has the opportunity to hear what is being said."

"And I have been brought up to express myself," interjected Daphne haughtily.

"I've sat here every day, seething, and every day it gets worse and worse. The anger is making my throat hurt and I want to scream and swear," Brenda looked at Rajesh plaintively. "What should I do?"

"Please," the guide gestured to Brenda with his open palm, "express your anger."

"Pardon?" Poor Brenda looked like a rabbit trapped in the headlights.

"Please. Express your anger. Scream, swear."

Brenda looked tentatively around the group who were watching the events unfold with fascination. She looked at John, seeming to ask for his permission and he gave her a hesitant nod. She sat quite still for a moment then threw back her head.

"Ahhhh!" she screamed. "Ahhhh! Fuck! Fuck! Fuck! Shut the fuck up! Ahhhh!" Brenda let go of her anger completely, drumming her feet on the floor as she screamed. "Ahhhh!"

The storm continued for maybe a minute then she composed herself and looked at the guide with a smile of wonderment on her face. "Oh! It worked! It worked! I feel so much better. All of the anger has gone! Thank you, Rajesh!"

"You're most welcome, Brenda," replied the guide, as tranquil as ever.

"Well done, Honey," said John, patting her arm, looking as though he didn't quite know how to react to this new development.

"Don't worry, Sweetie," she reassured him, intuitively. "It's only one of my personalities."

"Brenda, I for one can say how happy I am that you have been able to process all that anger," added Daphne, condescendingly. "Very unhealthy to keep it bottled up like that. Difficult childhood, was it?"

Brenda smiled at her, unruffled, no trace of anger remaining, but Lily and Stella couldn't contain themselves and burst into laughter. Soon the laughter rippled around the whole group, with even Daphne joining in. She was far too thick-skinned to be aware that her behaviour was the cause of their mirth.

What an extraordinary afternoon, thought Lily, wiping tears of laughter from her eyes. Despite the absurdity of the situation, it seemed to have brought the group closer. Brenda's courage had inspired her to believe that it might be possible to drop her masks after all. If a quiet little middle-aged lady could dare to be so real, then surely she could, too?

The guide clapped his hands, looking pleased. "That was a very good example of experiencing your feelings fully. Now, let us continue with our teaching."

Leaving the lounge, Lily found herself walking next to Scott and Marcie. She felt a little awkward but could hardly have gone rushing off like she had done earlier that day.

"Wasn't that wild! Brenda coming out with what the rest of us had been thinking all week," said Marcie, her eyes twinkling. "Oh, here she comes! I must go and congratulate her!" With that she dropped back, leaving Scott and Lily to walk on together.

"That was the funniest thing I've witnessed in a long time," said Scott, starting to snicker. "Poor old John! He didn't know how to react."

"I know," replied Lily, beginning to grin again at the recollection. "But the funniest thing was that Daphne still didn't understand how annoying she's been."

"Yeah, her skin's thicker than a rhino's butt."

"And you're intimately acquainted with rhinos' bottoms, are you?" said Lily teasingly.

"Well, there was this ex-girlfriend I had back in high school …"

"Now, now!" said Lily, primly. "We never speak ill of the exes."

"Quite. Thank you for your reprimand," said Scott with mock humility. "Nice to see you smiling, by the way."

"Yes … sorry about earlier. I wasn't feeling quite myself," Lily said, feeling a blush rising in her cheeks.

"Well, as long as you're OK now," he said quickly, not wishing to embarrass her. "What are you doing after the blessing session? Some of us are going to have a barbeque on the beach."

"Oh, I think I'll have an early night," she replied. "I really think I need a good night's sleep. Thanks, anyway."

"Well, if you change your mind … Stella's coming."

Lily smiled but didn't answer. She knew they'd have a great evening at the beach but she couldn't be around Scott. He clearly didn't have any idea of her attraction to him, thank goodness, but even so she would prefer to protect her heart. That would be done much more easily if she kept out of his way. If only she hadn't let herself fall for him.

"Oh! I think I've left my notebook in the lounge," she said suddenly. "I'll nip back and get it. See you later!"

Lily hurried back along the path to the lounge, knowing full well she hadn't forgotten her book but wanting to put some distance between herself and the American. She reached the reception and flopped down on the couch to gather her thoughts for a few minutes. There were only two more full days left and then she would be returning home. She had had such a wonderful experience being on this trip. She'd made some great new friendships, enjoyed the pleasures of being at a luxury resort on an idyllic island and had the most meaningful spiritual experience of her life. And it wasn't over yet. Lily smiled to herself; she wouldn't let a little unrequited love get her down. Her humour restored, she stretched and, rising from the couch, started to make her way back to the main bure. The evening blessing session wasn't due to start for half an hour or so, but she thought she'd get there early to spend a few moments soaking up that tranquil atmosphere.

She was ambling along, enjoying the beauty all around her when Rod appeared out of the bushes in front of her, making her jump.

"Taking a short cut from my bure. Didn't see me coming, did you?"

"No," said Lily, a little disconcerted. "I was daydreaming."

"Yes, you women never pay attention. Good thing I'm not a pervert."

"No ..." she replied, not so sure that he didn't fit that

description. The way he was looking at her legs was making her a little uncomfortable.

"I cut through the bushes because I wanted to ask you something," he continued, walking unnecessarily close. "I thought we might go for a moonlit stroll on the beach later this evening." He leered at her expectantly.

Dear God! Don't let the revulsion show on my face, thought Lily, flabbergasted that Rod could believe she would even consider his proposal. Be firm and not apologetic, she told herself, otherwise he'll think he's still in with a chance.

"Thanks, Rod, but I'm having any early night. The rest of our group is having a barbeque on the beach. I'm sure they'd be happy for you to join them," she replied resolutely.

Rod clearly wasn't used to being rebuffed. "Please yourself," he barked, increasing his pace and striding off, his shoulders stiff with displeasure. Lily slowed her pace, allowing some distance to form between them, once again amazed by the man's rudeness. Well, it's all happening this week, she thought. A mini soap-opera on the island of Pele. Perhaps she should write some of it into her book when she got home. The thought amused her and she started to form exaggerated caricatures to people her story. Her experiences this week could fill pages! She laughed out loud. Would anyone believe her? It was true: life was often more fantastic than fiction.

Reaching the main bure, she slipped inside. Though there wasn't any music playing yet, the candles were lit and an other-worldly atmosphere pervaded the place. It reminded her of a little chapel she had come across while on a skiing holiday in the French Alps. The tiny building was perched high up in the mountains and would often have been cut off in the depth of winter when the snowfall was at its heaviest. Lily's curiosity had made her venture in to explore further. What had made people erect a chapel in such a far-flung location? She had sat down on one of the hard wooden benches at the back of the crude building, reading the plaques on the wall that honoured the family who had dedicated the land and money for the chapel to be built. So that the cowherds may have a place to worship when they bring their beasts to high pasture read the inscription. Such an act of dedication, a sense of connection to something greater than themselves, she had thought and, although Lily was not a Catholic herself, she had been moved by the spirit of love that had created the place and that still lingered there.

Maybe it is reaching beyond ourselves that allows grace to flow, pondered Lily. She thought again about the events of the week; how, when she had allowed herself to let down her guard and open up to people's kindness, she had experienced a sense of connection that had been missing from her life. Perhaps divinity comes to us in ways we don't expect and often don't recognise, she thought. It's difficult, when life is so hectic, to take time out to look for the coincidences or hidden messages that are interwoven through life. Lily hoped that she would be able to take just a little of what she had experienced during her time on Pele so that she could share it with her family and friends. It was so good to be feeling a sense of ease at being herself and she wanted the people she cared about to experience the same relief and peace.

She heard the door behind her opening and looked around to see Stella slipping quietly into the room. Stella smiled at her friend then went to the sound system and put on the same track Lily had heard during their first meeting in the hall. Its haunting melody caused the heavenly atmosphere in the room to deepen perceptibly, awakening in Lily a sense of expectation for that evening's blessing.

"This is the Moola Mantra," said Stella, sliding into the seat next to her friend. "It's one of my favourites."

Om Sat Chit Ananda Parabrahma
Purushothama Paramatma
Sri Bhagavathi Sametha
Sri Bhagavathe Namaha

"It's beautiful," said Lily. "What does it mean?"

"It is inviting The Divine to manifest itself here with us; it's like calling its name. It invokes all aspects of divinity, spirit or energy – whatever you like to call it: the primordial sound of the universe; formless, shapeless existence; pure consciousness; the loving, friendly, blissful aspect of the divine; the supreme, absolute being; the guiding energy force that dwells in each of us and the masculine and feminine expressions of divinity."

"Phew! That's quite mind-blowing! I'd never thought of God being so dynamic," said Lily.

"No, we've reduced divinity to something small-minded and petty, a grumpy old man," agreed Stella. "We've lost sight of the beauty and magnificence of creation and forgotten that it's only a dim reflection of the force that created it."

The two women sat quietly, letting the music flow over them. Gradually, the hall filled up and, after a few more minutes, the Oneness Beings took their seats at the front of the room, assisted by the guides. The room was lost in meditation, drinking in the atmosphere, little by little letting go of distracting thoughts. Then the guides began to call people forward as before to receive the blessing. Lily and Stella were seated at the rear of the room this time, so it would be a little while before they would be invited to go up. Lily sat with her eyes closed, enjoying the tranquillity for a while, feeling a deepening sense of connection with herself and the magnificence of the divinity that was revealed through the Moola Mantra. When she was called forward for her blessing, she felt a tremor of joy as though she was going to be reunited with a dear friend. As the first Oneness Being touched her head, she felt a deep sense of being known and loved that filled her heart with wonder. She moved to receive the second blessing and the feeling deepened. Lily had always heard religious people saying that God was love, but she had never experienced the reality of that love before. It was as though every part of her was laid bare and she knew there was no need to hide; she was embraced and loved, just as she was. It finally dawned on her that she could begin to love herself, that she deserved to be loved, just because she was Lily. A tear ran down her cheek and, as she made her way over to the bean-bags to be still and absorb the experience, the vision of a butterfly emerging from its chrysalis passed through her mind as clear as a photograph.

She sat with her eyes closed for a long time. She hadn't appreciated just how long it had been until one of the guides touched her arm gently and she opened her eyes; she was the last person left in the hall.

"I'm so sorry," she began, struggling to her feet.

"There is no need to be," replied the young man, smiling. "Sometimes after the blessing, people are in rapture all night. Have a peaceful evening."

Leaving the meeting hall, she glanced at her watch: 8:35 p.m. The group would be down at the beach, having their barbeque. Maybe it would be fun to join them, after all.

Chapter 14

Lily ran quickly back to the bure, changed into her shorts and T-shirt, then headed towards the ocean. Laughter floated back on the evening breeze as she crossed the sand. Scott and Tom were in charge of the barbeque and the others were sitting on beach towels laughing about the day's events. She counted seven people; Rod and Daphne were missing.

"I was so amazed that Rajesh wasn't shocked or offended by me swearing,"Brenda was saying. She was cuddled up next to John, looking as carefree as a young girl. He had his arm around her and was gazing at her fondly. Her break-through had clearly had a wider effect; they seemed much more in balance as a couple. John was encouraging her to express herself instead of always taking the lead.

"Yes," agreed Gina. "He reminded me of the stories I've read about the Buddha, who never passed judgment on anyone. He just accepted people as they were, knowing there is always a reason why we act the way we do."

"Hi, Lily! Come and sit over here," said John, squeezing up closer to Brenda.

"Hey, Lily! Glad you could join us. What would you like to drink?" called Tom from the barbeque.

"Hi, everybody!" Lily felt herself going pink with pleasure at the warmth of their greeting. "Just some fruit juice would be nice. Mango, if you have it." She settled herself on the blanket, next to John.

"Coming right up!" Tom poured a tall glass of freshly-juiced mango and Scott brought it over.

"Glad you changed your mind," he smiled, handing it to her.

"Me too," she replied. "It would be a shame to miss the opportunity of spending the evening with such a great bunch of people."

"Hear, hear!" said Stella, raising her glass.

"Hear, hear!"

The group raised their glasses in a salute to each other. It reminded Lily of the reception at the beginning of the week and she started to laugh.

"What's so funny?" said Stella. "Do tell."

"I was thinking of that welcome party on the mainland," replied Lily. "I couldn't stand the sight of any of you and wished there was some way that I could get back on an aircraft and fly home. I don't feel like that now, of course," she added hastily, starting to blush. "I feel as though you're dear friends that I've known for ages."

"What made you feel like that?" asked Gina, in surprise.

"I suppose I didn't like myself much, though I didn't realise it at the time and was subconsciously terrified that you wouldn't like me either," said Lily, pensively. "I didn't know what I was doing; it may seem more bearable to shut people out before they reject you, but it makes for a lonely existence."

"You're a great girl," said Marcie, quietly. "Nobody could help liking you."

"Thank you," said Lily, trying to keep the surprise out of her voice. How strange life was, she thought. If you just gave people a chance, the good in them would usually surface.

"We all love you, Lily," said Stella, blowing her a kiss from across the small fire they had lit to keep them warm.

"Stop, stop!" Lily raised her hand. "You'll make me cry. Come on Stella! Haven't you got an inappropriate story to lift this serious atmosphere?"

"Absolutely, darling!" she addressed the group. "Would you like to hear about the time I had a divine visitation during sex? Wonderful!" she continued, not waiting for a reply. "After I lost my wonderful husband I was sad for the longest time. Eventually, I realised I needed to start living a full life again, not only for the boys but for myself. And so, naturally, shortly after that my thoughts turned to sex," she said, her eyes twinkling. "I wasn't ready for a serious relationship but, as a woman has needs, I started to consider who might be suitable for the role of Friend with Benefits. Sorry to embarrass you, John," she interjected, seeing him turning scarlet in the light of the fire. "Anyway, I had an old friend, who we'll call Fred, who I'd known for about ten years. He'd always had a major crush on me and I thought it might work out well for both of us." She giggled at the recollection. "I really should have known better. Fred was a loyal, dependable sort but it didn't generate a lot of va va voom in the bedroom. The trouble was, he got it into his head that it was going to be a weekly rendezvous, and that alone would have been enough to kill any sense of passion in me. I like spontaneity, surprise, a bit of being thrown around the bedroom."

"What! A quiet girl like you!" bantered Scott.

"Don't interrupt! Now, where was I? Oh, yes," she continued. "Poor old Fred kept turning up every Wednesday night at ten o'clock, when the boys were asleep, clutching a bunch of carnations – the dreariest flowers in the world! It was making me quite depressed but I didn't have the heart to let him know that I didn't want to carry on with the arrangement," she sighed. "So, let me set the scene. My beautiful antique bed has a deep head-board where I kept the remote control for the television. Being single again, I had moved the portable into the bedroom to keep me company at night. One Wednesday evening, Fred was doing his thing and I was lying there underneath him, feeling totally absent, when the remote flew off the shelf and hit me between the eyes. I just couldn't stop laughing and, in the end, dear old Fred got offended and climbed off in a huff." Stella grinned. "He would have been even more offended if he'd known that, just as the remote hit me, I heard The Divine's voice in my head shouting, 'CHANGE THE CHANNEL'!!! We never had sex again!"

The group erupted, including John who had looked as if he

wasn't quite sure whether it was a politically-correct subject to be discussing. Next to him, Brenda was laughing so much there were tears running down her face.

"Poor guy!" said Tom, shaking his head in sympathy. "We men get a raw deal. We try to provide a service and it's thrown back in our faces."

"Talking of raw, Honey," said Gina, "What's taking so long with the barbeque? I'm starving!"

The atmosphere had developed into one of easy companionship. The friends were chatting quietly together or enjoying the view of the moonlit ocean. Lily took her plate of food and went over to Marcie at the other side of the fire.

"Hey! Sit down," said the young woman, patting the space next to her on the blanket. "It's been a good evening, hasn't it?"

"It has," agreed Lily. "I'm glad I changed my mind and came along. Thank you for what you said earlier, by the way."

"I was a bit hard on you at the beginning of the week," replied Marcie honestly. "I was taking my frustrations out on everyone else." They concentrated on their food for the next few moments and then Lily tentatively spoke again.

"It's nice to see you and Scott are getting along so well."

"Yes, if a little ironic," sighed Marcie.

"Oh?"

"We split up a few days ago. Hardly anyone knows but I'm sure I can trust you not to say anything. You English are so discreet."

"I'm really sorry!" exclaimed Lily, feeling extremely tactless.

"Don't be. I'm not. Scott's not. At first I was afraid and acted like a spoiled prima donna to hide my feelings. The morning after we'd decided to split, I screamed and shouted, blamed Scott for everything and even threw the cafetière at him." Lily raised her eyebrows.

"I know," said Marcie, seeing her look. "Outrageous behaviour, but I was suddenly really scared of losing everything. Scott normally placates me when I lose my temper but he shouted back, told me to stop being such a brat, said I didn't want him and I needed to get over my bruised ego. I was furious because he was spot on. I raged about the bure while he was out sailing with you guys, furious because he hadn't bought into my drama." She shrugged. "I tried to hold on to my temper but without him there to shout at, I calmed down and faced up to the fact he was telling the truth. It wasn't what I wanted to see at first, I was so involved in my need to be right, but it doesn't seem possible to hold on to all that negative energy around here. I felt so relieved to think that I would not to be going through the motions any more."

"I understand that. It took me a while to face up to it, but my husband and I had been living an illusion, almost from the start of our relationship. Once I finally saw it, there was no going back," said Lily.

"Yeah. If you're prepared to see the truth, it will set you free," paraphrased Marcie. "So, what's been your story this week?"

"Lots of relationship stuff," replied Lily. "Realising I'd never let myself grieve for my marriage ending. You know, that whole British stiff upper-lip, don't show any emotion. And I've finally been able to see my mother as she is, letting go of old presumptions. Hopefully, I'll be able to let her be herself now and maybe she'll be able to do the same for me."

"One of the things Ananda Giri said this morning that really struck me was that the greatest gift you can give someone is allowing them to be themselves," said Marcie. "I never wanted to see Scott as he truly is; I was always trying to encourage him to make more money, when that's not what drives him; he's a people person. It's me that has always been motivated by money," she smiled disparagingly. "New Jersey born and raised – and terrified

I'd end up back there."

Lily nodded thoughtfully. "Most of the time we have no idea what's driving us, what we're doing to ourselves and other people," she said thoughtfully. "We have so many expectations of how life is supposed to be: do well at school; get a good job; find a partner; have babies, make sure they grow up healthy and give them every chance you can of happiness and success; retire and enjoy your free time, at last; finally, we die. We get on that merry-go-round and don't take the time to ask if we're actually going anywhere or where it might be that we want to go. It usually takes something big like illness, death or divorce to make us think about what we truly want."

"And what do you truly want?" asked Marcie, her expression curious.

Lily sat quietly, contemplating the question, before she replied. "You know, I just want to enjoy being me, as I am, without all the pre-conceived ideas about what I should think, or how I should act. Listening to Ananda Giri and being around the guides has made me think that life would be much more meaningful if I was who I really am and allowed other people to be themselves, too, instead of trying to make them fit my ideas of who they should be, what they should do," she smiled in surprise. "I'd never really thought about that before. I always thought I'd be fulfilled when I found the right man, was successful in my career, had a family but, although these are good things, they don't make you complete. It's nice to finally understand that I am already enough – more than enough – as I am; I just need to remember that."

"That's a nice way of looking at things," said Marcie. "Not expecting others to complete you would take the pressure off them – and you."

"It's so simple but it makes so much sense, doesn't it?" replied Lily, smiling happily. "I wonder if it ever would have occurred to me if I hadn't come here."

"Maybe, but I think it would have taken a lot longer to get there," reasoned Marcie. "Like you said, being around the guides is a much more powerful message than anything they've actually said. They have no agenda, apart from spreading a message of Oneness and healing; they embody everything they say in the way they interact between themselves and with us; they are totally accepting, which helps us to realise we are fine just the way we are. You can find that concept in hundreds of self-development books but it really makes an impact when you see people living it."

"That's very insightful," said Lily. "You've really thought about it."

"It's the lawyer in me," Marcie replied. "To be honest with you, the main reason I came to this seminar was to network. It's second-nature to me, to make contacts that I can benefit from; the spiritual part was secondary for me. I thought we'd do a bit of yoga and have some meditation which, along with the spa, would have been a welcome combination to help me unwind a little, it's been a crazy year." She continued, "As soon as I saw that the teaching was more structured than the usual airy-fairy stuff, I was a little wary. I started to process what was going on, as though I was going to present evidence in court. It's habit; I have a very analytical mind and I despise charlatans – but I couldn't find any incongruence between who they were and what they taught. It's their authenticity that really got to me. Normally I never discuss personal stuff with strangers but I spilled all my secrets to Rajesh like a teenage girl writing in her secret journal."

"Strange, isn't it?" said Lily. "I did the same. I think that I just felt safe."

"Safe," echoed Marcie. "That's it. I felt really safe for the first time since who knows when, knowing I wasn't going to be judged or taken advantage of."

"I really like the image they present of The Divine, spirit, the universe – whatever you want to call it," said Lily. "My grandparents used to take me to church with them when I was little. I could never understand how they could say in one breath that God was love but then, in the next, talk about damnation. It never made sense to me."

"We've tried to fit something infinite into our own small, limited model of the world and distorted it with our ignorance and fears," replied Marcie, "but I'm with Einstein– the universe is a friendly place."

She yawned. "All this fresh air and philosophising is wearing me out. I think I'm going to hit the hay. Scottie!" she called, getting up, "I'm turning in. Stay here, have fun. See you later, English," she said to Lily, "good to talk to you."

"You too." Lily watched Marcie pick her way carefully across the pebbly sand and disappear into the trees. What an extraordinary young woman. She wasn't sure that she could have been so gracious under the circumstances. Probably would have gone straight home to lick my wounds, she thought. Good for Marcie, for not giving up on the trip. She was right; it did seem difficult to hold on to negativity in this atmosphere. Maybe it wasn't a bad place to end a relationship, if that's where it was heading; all those blessings definitely seemed to have a healing effect.

"Nice to see you two have made friends." Stella sat down next to her friend. "Did she tell you? She and Scott broke up."

Lily laughed. "And she thinks the English are discreet!"

"She knows I know," said Stella, dismissively, "but you're right, I don't understand where anyone got the notion that the English are discreet. Have they never seen Stephen Fry present the BAFTAs? So you knew already?"

"Yes, she's just told me," said Lily. "She seems very composed. Scott does, too. It's never easy breaking up, is it? I'm glad it's not been too traumatic for either of them."

"Most of the time the trauma comes from not facing the fact that it's over," said Stella.

"Yes, we're not always very good at letting go, are we?"

"Better the devil you know, and all that," Stella agreed. "Would you like some more chicken? OK, let's see what's left on the barbeque."

The two of them went to see what was left to eat. "What can we get you, girls?" asked Tom. He and Scott were still in charge of the cooking, though most people's appetites were beginning to flag.

"We're going to have some chicken, darling, but leave it to Scott and come with me. Gina wants a word with you," said Stella, dragging him away.

"But I've just spoken to Gina," he protested.

"I know, but she forgot to ask you something. I'm just giving romance a helping hand," she continued in a whisper. "Scott and Lily need to be left alone."

"Stella!" Tom groaned. "You're incorrigible!"

Chapter 15

"I'm Tom's sous-chef really," Scott was saying to Lily. "He's a little reticent about handing over control of the tongs, but I'll try my best not to burn the chicken."

"Poor Tom! Blaming him for your inferiority in the kitchen while he's not here to defend himself. Shame on you!" she mocked.

"Found out again! You're a hard one to slip anything by," he said, feigning dismay.

"Watch out! It's turning black!" squealed Lily. "You're a hopeless chef!"

"True!" Scott held up the singed carcass. "Tom!" he shouted. "I declare myself fired! You better come back and take over. Do you want anything else to eat?" he asked her.

She shook her head. "For some strange reason, I seem to have lost my appetite."

"Good. Come for a walk with me. The fishing boats go out at about this time. They're worth seeing. The fleet hasn't changed for hundreds of years; the boats are still made in the same local tradition that has been passed down for centuries."

"Oh! Shall we see if anyone else wants to come?" asked Lily, feeling awkward about going off alone with Scott.

"Sure. Listen up guys," he said, addressing the group. "I'm going to show Lily the fishing fleet. Do any of you want to come along?"

"The three of us have seen them head out countless times," said Stella, "but you must see them, Lily. It's quite a spectacle."

"John, Brenda?"

Lily was relieved that the couple said they would love to come along. The four of them set off across the sand, Scott and Lily walking ahead and John and Brenda following, their arms entwined, enjoying their new-found appreciation of each other.

Lily walked quietly by Scott's side. She wanted to offer him her condolences but was distracted by being in such close proximity to him, feeling very conscious of his presence. He moved with ease, his movements powerful and fluid. Like many sportsmen, he seemed to know and respect his strength and carried himself with quiet confidence. She felt like a little Burmese cat tripping along beside a panther, both protected and vulnerable. Glancing at him in the moonlight, his hair dishevelled by the warm evening breeze, her mind again conjured up the image of Heathcliffe in Wuthering Heights. The awareness of her attraction to Scott struck her suddenly like a physical blow, taking away her breath.

"Are you OK?" Scott asked her, hearing her gasp.

"I thought I felt something dart across my foot," lied Lily. "Probably a gecko."

"Oooh! Are there lizards on the beach?" Brenda's voice drifted across the quiet night air.

"Lizards or crabs, Honey," replied John. "Tell you what, I'll give you a piggy-back. Hop up." Giggling, Brenda accepted his gallant offer and jumped on. John trotted past as though she weighed no more than a child, the pair of them laughing in glee, caught up in the pleasure of the moment.

"Come on then," said Scott, stooping slightly in invitation to Lily. "We can't let them have all the fun. Jump on."

She hesitated for a split-second and then leapt up, wrapping her arms around his neck. They raced across the sand, drawing level with the older couple, whooping and laughing.

"Come on, Honey! Don't let him beat you!" squealed Brenda and her husband bravely rose to the challenge, increasing his stride.

"You have to let him win," Lily whispered in Scott's ear, "but he can't know."

Scott nodded his head almost imperceptibly and they ran, neck and neck, towards the stone wall that marked the entrance to the port.

Lily felt exhilarated; for the next few minutes she and Scott were a team. She had thrown caution to the wind and was enjoying the moment, the sense of his strength, the smell of his skin, their conspiracy to throw the race. She hadn't been able to resist his offer of a piggy-back ride and hadn't wanted to. There was no mischief in it; they were with John and Brenda and it was just harmless fun. Scott would never know how she felt about him and this would be her only indulgence; she'd make sure that no similar incident occurred.

"Get ready," Scott hissed over his shoulder, "I'm going to bail."

He drew slightly ahead of John, who was breathing heavily. They were a short distance from the wall when Scott stumbled and fell to his knees, allowing John to pull ahead. Lily clung on like a limpet until Scott hit the sand, then relaxed her grip and slid the short distance on to the sand. Lying on her back, overcome with giggles, she looked up to see that John and Brenda had climbed the short flight of steps up on to the top of the port wall and were doing a victory dance.

"You did it, Honey! You're my hero!" cried Brenda triumphantly and embraced him passionately.

"Well, things have certainly livened up for those two," said Scott, rolling on to his side to face Lily.

"It's great to see them so happy and carefree," she said, watching them. "Brenda was so timid when she first got here and John just seemed to take her for granted.

"Not any more," grinned Scott. "That kiss would make some teenagers blush."

"How lovely!" said Lily. "A little romance. It's what distinguishes a couple from being companions or lovers. I was always coming across my parents kissing when I was a teenager. It used to make me cringe, I thought they were too old for all that. Now I can see that they loved each other so much it kept their passion alive. No wonder she misses him."

Lily looked away from the touching scene to find Scott watching her silently. His face was inches away, partially shadowed so that she couldn't quite read the expression in his eyes.

"What's up?" she said, attempting to lighten the atmosphere.

"You have sand on your face," he replied and, reaching out his hand, he wiped it gently away.

They looked at each other steadily for a moment, then Scott rolled on to his knees and rose to his feet. He offered Lily his hand, pulling her up and, without speaking, they climbed the steps on to the port wall, where they found Brenda and John watching the small fishing fleet leaving on its nightly expedition.

"It's so cute," murmured Brenda, watching the tiny craft rowing out to sea, their lights bobbing.

"Isn't it?" agreed Lily, grateful for the couple's presence. She felt torn between relief and sadness that the poignant moment between her and Scott had passed, but knew that it had to. Neither of them would want to hurt Marcie and if they let anything develop between them it would be unavoidable. The irony of having had such a strong connection with a man like Scott, when nothing could come of it, would normally have left Lily feeling desolate, but she felt quite calm. She knew now that the attraction between them wasn't her imagination and, although it contradicted her baser instincts, she was prepared to let this chance for happiness go. After today, she had a pervading sense of being looked after and knew she didn't have to cling to this moment. There would be others.

Scott spotted Nelson a little further down the wall watching the fishermen depart and went to join him. He was shocked by what had just happened between him and Lily and needed some distance to put it in perspective.

"Evening Mr Scott," Nelson's greeting was warm; he had

known Scott for almost as long as Stella and was fond of him.

"Hello, Nelson. A good evening for the fleet, do you think?"

"Mmm," mused the old man. "Hard to say. There's a storm forecast. The fish will move to deeper water."

The two men exchanged a few words in conversation, then lapsed into silence, watching as the boats were gradually swallowed by darkness. In the silence, Scott's thoughts had started to clamour for attention again.

He couldn't believe that he hadn't realised he had feelings for Lily. Tom had hinted as much earlier that day but he had been completely in denial, preferring to believe that she was a welcome breath of fresh air after all the drama between him and Marcie. He had nearly kissed her down on the beach just now, an impulse that had been so sudden and strong he'd barely been able to resist it. Racing across the beach had been so light-hearted and playful, a moment of sheer happiness. Sharing it with Lily had been perfect. As they'd lain laughing on the sand, it was as though the mist had cleared and he had understood the truth: he wanted her in his life. The timing was absolutely terrible; he still cared deeply for Marcie and wouldn't do anything that would hurt her. It would be completely inappropriate to be pursuing Lily in these circumstances and, anyway, she would be flying back to England in a couple of days. Finally, the underlying stress of the last few days kicked in and Scott felt incredibly weary. He sighed. He would have to go and join the others and behave with some semblance of normality. It wouldn't be easy when there was so much he wanted to say to Lily. Looking back along the port wall, he saw two figures silhouetted in the moonlight; Lily had gone.

Stella let herself back into the bure and was surprised to see light shining from Lily's room. She put her head around the door.

"Hello! You came back early. Everything OK?" she asked, looking anxious.

Lily put down The Alchemist and smiled. "Yes, everything's fine. It was lovely to see the boats going out, I felt as though I'd drifted back in time."

"Yes, it's magical, isn't it? Though I wouldn't like to venture out to sea in one of those tiny crafts. Brenda and John came back a while ago. I thought you might have gone for a walk with Scott."

Lily shook her head, amused by Stella's obvious disappointment. "No, I wanted a little time to myself, to think about everything that's happened this week."

"So you didn't spend any time with Scott on your own?"

"Stella!" Lily pretended to scold her friend. "Anyone would think you'd been trying to match-make."

"Well, of course I'm trying to match-make!" exclaimed Stella, plonking herself down on the edge of Lily's bed, her face a picture of exasperation. "You and Scott would be perfect for each other."

"It would hardly be very sensitive, me and Scott spending time together when he and Marcie have just split up."

"Aha!" Stella pounced. "So you admit you like him."

Lily blushed. "Whether I do or not is irrelevant; nothing's going to happen."

Stella folded her arms and looked at her friend speculatively. "But something has happened, I can tell. What was it?"

Lily recounted the story of the piggy-back race, pausing at the part where she and Scott had tumbled on to the sand.

"And?" Stella prompted her, impatiently.

"Well… I think he was going to kiss me."

"And why didn't he? What was he waiting for?"

"He could hardly start snogging me with Brenda and John in full view!" retorted Lily. "Hardly anyone knows that he and Marcie have split up and, if they did, I'd imagine they'd think it was pretty crass to be so insensitive."

"Yes, but you could be discreet about it," Stella persisted.

"No," said Lily firmly. "I didn't come here to find a man, Stell. Joining UPG was an opportunity for me to find out who I am and what I want for my life. I've loved these last few days, it's been so much more than I was expecting: meeting everyone, having so much fun, listening to the guides. I'm so happy, I feel as though I'm really starting to enjoy who I am for the first time. I don't want to be distracted by getting fixated on a man and missing out on all the opportunities that are here for me. Believe me, I've done that before, completely losing sight of what I wanted by getting caught up in trying to please the guy. I don't want to do that again."

"Well, you seem very sure, very composed," said her friend reluctantly.

Lily smiled. "I am. I feel as though I had a big shift today in understanding what will make me happy. Believe me, lying there so close to Scott, I could have let him know that I wanted him to kiss me and he would have done. It would have caused so much unhappiness and awkwardness. I didn't want to spend the next couple of days sneaking about, consumed by guilt, too distracted to be able to focus on the teaching." She rubbed her nose pensively. "I know this might sound a bit silly, but I just feel as though my life is so rich right now that I don't have to grab hold of Scott as though he's my last chance for happiness." She stretched out her arms in a joyful gesture of abundance. "There's a whole world of opportunity out there."

"Wow! I'll have some of what you're having," said Stella, admiringly. "Good for you! You're really starting to know what you want."

"I am, aren't I?" replied Lily, grinning happily. "Though I will say it's very good for my ego to know that a man as gorgeous as Scott would be interested in me."

"Don't be ridiculous!" chided Stella. "You're delightful! Any man should consider it a privilege to be with you. Don't go spoiling your new-found freedom with that attitude!"

"Thank you," agreed Lily. "Another old belief to let go of. I am a work-in-progress."

"Aren't we all, darling?" replied Stella, dropping a kiss on her cheek as she stood up. "Aren't we all?"

Chapter 16

Scott woke as the early morning light began to seep through the blinds. He glanced at his watch: 5:34 a.m. He was wide awake, as he had been for much of the night. Thankfully, Marcie had slept through all of his tossing and turning; she was lying on her side, peaceful in sleep, her breathing rising and falling gently. He shrugged off a slight feeling of envy and sat up. There was no point lying there, he knew he wouldn't be able to go back to sleep now. It was still cool enough to allow him to go for a run; he got dressed quietly and stepped out into the welcoming sunlight. Another day in paradise; his spirits lifted at the sight of his beautiful surroundings. He was glad he'd decided to get up and do something constructive rather than moping in bed. Following the narrow beach path to the end, Scott found himself on the pale golden sand and broke into a run.

He soon slipped into the familiar rhythm, his body like a high-performance car that responded easily to the challenge being asked of it. The motion seemed to bring order to the thoughts that had been bouncing around his head like bumper-cars all night; he was feeling much more resourceful. He had got over his surprise at the strength of feelings he had for Lily and he was able to look at the situation more objectively. Of course, he wasn't going to be insensitive to Marcie but he wasn't prepared to lose contact with Lily. He knew that he would do whatever it took to get to know her better and find out if there was any chance of them being together. He would have to look out for the opportunity to speak to her before the seminar ended. He felt confident there would be one; he didn't think it was a coincidence that he had met this woman, even if he'd been slow to recognise the fact at first. No, things would work out for them, for Marcie, too. Feeling invigorated by his new-found optimism, Scott increased his pace, sprinting across the sand, the morning sun as bright as his frame of mind.

"Hey, Scott! How's it going, buddy?" Tom's greeting floated down from the rear balcony of the bure. "Good run?"

"Excellent!" called Scott, "really helped me clear my head. You got a minute?"

"Sure," replied his friend. "Come on up."

Scott flopped down on to a chair and stretched out his long legs. "Nice view from here."

"Yeah. I watched you run along the beach and right around the harbour," said Tom. "I found it quite tiring."

"You always were an armchair sportsman," laughed Scott.

"Listen, I've got four crazy children to run around with," was Tom's retort. "That keeps me fit enough."

"Touché. You missing them?"

"Of course," he replied. "We're really looking forward to seeing them but they're down on the farm with Grandma, not missing us at all as Jake so kindly told us when we phoned last night."

"Kids!" said Scott, shaking his head. "No social graces."

"Their honesty can be a little brutal at times," grinned Tom. "They don't take any prisoners. But enough about my tribe. What's going on with you?"

"You know that conversation we had yesterday about Lily?" said Scott, coming straight to the point. "I've realised that I like her." To his surprise, Tom stood up and made to go back into the bure. "What's up?" asked Scott, perplexed. "Where are you going?"

"One of those conversations is about as much as I can take," he said over his shoulder. "Sorry to cut short your lie-in, Honey," he called through the bure's open patio door. "Scott needs to talk to you."

After a couple of minutes, his wife appeared wrapped in a robe, her hair still dishevelled from sleep.

"Morning, Scottie," said Gina sleepily, stretching up on tip-toes to receive his hug. "And what's so important that you had to drag me from my slumber?" she asked, seating herself on her husband's lap. "It's a good thing for both of you that the blessing has calmed down my hormones and the evil twin has packed her bags."

"Scott likes Lily," said Tom.

"And?" Gina looked at Tom enquiringly. "Why did you feel the need to get me out of bed for that news?" She smiled at Scott. "I already knew."

"That's why we needed you," said Tom, defending himself. "You always pick up on what's going on and you give such good advice."

"How did you know I liked her?" asked Scott, looking baffled. "I only worked it out myself last night."

"Scottie! I've known you half my life," laughed Gina. "Probably no-one else would have picked up on it, but it was just the way you looked at her."

"What d'you mean?" said Scott, sounding worried.

"Oh, don't worry, it wasn't a love-sick school-boy look," said Gina quickly, to alleviate his dismay. "When she was talking to you, you could see that you were completely absorbed, like you were the only people on the planet. She was the same, too. It was blindingly obvious to me." Gina looked bemused. "I don't know why other people don't notice these things."

"I'm glad they don't!" exclaimed Scott, a bit embarrassed. "Talk about feeling exposed. You're not one of those psychics, are you?" he added, suspiciously.

"No," she grinned, "but my family did originally come from Salem."

Scott regarded the tiny redhead for a few seconds, his look a mixture of admiration and bemusement, before continuing. "Obviously, I know the situation is a bit delicate, with Marcie and me just having split up. I don't want to do anything to hurt Marcie and I don't want Lily to think I'm an insensitive bastard. How do I handle this without anyone getting hurt?"

"It won't be a problem, I'm sure," said Gina, confidently. "Lily definitely likes you – I think you'd be adorable together, by the way – but obviously you need to be considerate to Marcie. She's been really brave, staying on here and she really seems to be enjoying the process." She frowned. "She is only human, though, and it would be a blow to her pride to think you were over her so quickly. She could easily slip back into lawyer mode and all the good she's gained from this week would be undone. I think you'll have to be patient for the moment." She was quiet, considering how best to help them when an idea struck her and her face lit up with a beaming smile.

"How about if I invite her over for Thanksgiving? They don't celebrate it in England, so she probably doesn't have any plans. You could come down, too, if your family could spare you. What do you think?"

"Gina! That's a great idea!" exclaimed Scott, picking her up off Tom's lap and spinning her around. "We were due to go to Marcie's family this year, so my folks weren't expecting us. You really are a star, you know."

"I know," replied Gina, revelling in Scott's excitement. "I'll speak to Lily and let her know the plan. If she opens up to me and doesn't mind me talking about it, I'll let you know what she says." Her hand flew to her stomach. "You'd better put me down now. The baby's showing its displeasure by kicking me in the ribs."

"Sorry, baby!" said Scott, kissing Gina's stomach as he put her down. "I'll make it up to you when you're out!"

"Great!" said Tom, winking at his wife. "We'll be sending the new edition up to New York to visit Uncle Scottie, every chance we get!"

Lily and Stella were sitting on their terrace, enjoying breakfast in the early morning sunshine. Nelson had taken to bringing them a selection of fruit and pastries from the restaurant's buffet, knowing that Stella wasn't a morning person and would rather miss breakfast than get up early. Lily was writing postcards while her friend sat quietly enjoying their peaceful corner of paradise, drinking in the sounds and fragrances as if it was her first visit.

"I could never get tired of this place," she sighed happily. "It's so magical."

"It really is," agreed Lily, "but part of the magic is that you haven't lost your appreciation for it."

"Mmmm," pondered Stella. "I suppose so. I guess it's the little girl in me; each time I catch the plane from the mainland, I feel as though I'm becoming part of a fairy tale. I'm always a bit surprised that it's mine. Don't get me wrong," she added in response to Lily's raised eyebrows, "there was plenty of money when I was a child but not a lot of emotional security. My mother's propensity for changing her husbands was very unsettling; not many of them were interested in me. The times I spent here were like my *Secret Garden*, you know that children's book? I feel as though this place has materialised out of my imagination and that, if I finally grow up, it might disappear."

"Not much chance of that," retorted Lily. "The playful child is still very much alive, looking for as much mischief as she can get away with."

Stella smiled happily in agreement, stretching her golden legs. "Talking about opportunities for mischief, here comes Daphne. Good morning!" she trilled.

"Good morning," replied the older woman, "I'm just doing a little exploring before breakfast. I didn't know this was your *bure*." She gazed at the pretty little house with envy. "You were lucky to get in here," she said to Lily, waspishly.

"I'm lucky to have her," responded Stella. "Won't you join us for breakfast?"

"Oooh. Breakfast delivered to your *bure*! What favouritism!" Daphne began to mount the steps. "Don't mind if I do."

"I'll bring out another chair," said Lily, getting up. She was sorry that the woman had taken Stella up on the invitation. Daphne's attitude grated on her as much as it had at the beginning of the week. Returning to the porch, she found that Daphne had installed herself in Lily's chair and was eating the last almond croissant, Lily's favourite. She felt a growing sense of annoyance but said nothing, seating herself on the little kitchen chair in a disgruntled mood.

"So what has been your experience of this week?" Stella was asking.

"Oh! It's been wonderful," cooed Daphne, wearing a pious expression. "I have studied with some of the greatest spiritual masters in my time and dear Ananda Giriji is certainly in that class."

"I thought his name was Ananda Giri?" said Lily, innocently.

Daphne gave her a disparagingly look. "The *ji* is a sign of respect but I wouldn't have expected you to know that."

"Why wouldn't you have expected me to know that?" asked Lily, her temper rising.

"Well, my dear, you're obviously new to the spiritual path." She turned to Stella again. "These croissants are excellent. I must have some sent to my *bure* tomorrow."

Lily was furious. So what if she was new to all this? And thank goodness she was! If being in those sorts of circles for years meant she would turn out like Daphne, she didn't want any part of it. Fuming silently, she wished she could deliver a cutting retort but she was too angry to think of one.

"And what has been the best part for you?" continued Stella.

"I particularly liked the way Rajeshji handled Brenda's outburst. So diplomatic, the way he didn't draw attention to her instability."

Lily was about to jump to Brenda's defence when Stella spoke again.

"No, Daphne. I want to know about you. What has happened this week that has really touched you? Personally."

"Well, I ..." The older woman looked uncomfortable and began to dab the linen napkin to her lips, avoiding Stella's steady gaze. "It's all been amazing. Just amazing." She glanced at her watch. "Is that the time? I need to get my notebook before the meeting starts. Thank you for breakfast, Stella. See you in the hall." With that, she left the table and hurried down the steps.

"Poor old Daphne," said Stella, watching the woman hasten away.

"What do you mean 'poor old Daphne'?" raged Lily. "The woman's a harpy! I wished Brenda had slapped her the other day, she would have got away with it. *I'd* like to slap her!"

"Dear me!" laughed Stella. "You have got yourself in a temper!"

"Of course I have! She's enough to drive anyone mad. And why didn't you tell her she was sitting in my chair?"

"Why didn't you tell her yourself?"

"Because I was so annoyed that I couldn't have trusted myself to speak."

"No, I can see that," agreed Stella. "You could breathe, by the way."

"What?" Lily was looking confused.

"You could breathe," repeated Stella. "You're so caught up in your annoyance that your chest has contracted. Just breathe."

Lily accepted that Stella was right and took a couple of deep breaths, calming herself.

"So what do you think it is about Daphne that pushes your buttons so hard?" asked Stella, looking at her friend appraisingly

"I don't know," said Lily shaking her head. "She's just reminds me of everyone in my life who has trampled over me as though I was nothing."

"But you behaved as though you were nothing," replied Stella, calmly. "You let her sit in your seat and eat your croissant without saying a word. I'm not trying to be hard on you," she said, responding to Lily's hurt look, "but you need to understand that the people that come into our lives bring us lessons. You are a lovely, funny, generous woman but you need to have clearer boundaries. You were ready to jump to Brenda's cause but you did nothing to protect your own. Perhaps that's the lesson Daphne's bringing you: people treat us the way we allow them to. As you continue to make distinctions about what is acceptable to you, it will start to be reflected in the way people treat you." She smiled. "Don't look so glum."

"I was feeling so together last night, so connected," protested Lily. "Now I've let that woman annoy me and I feel as though I've lost all the ground I'd gained this week."

"It's not that," said Stella. "Think of it this way: you've gained enough ground to allow you to deal with this situation and grow. Before you came here, you probably wouldn't have considered the possibility that there was something in you that was being triggered. You would have written Daphne off as an annoying old bat and reacted the same way to anyone else like her who crossed your path, continuing to carry around all that resentment, instead of doing something about it."

"It's not fair," said Lily, looking like a sulky child. "How come you get this stuff so easily?"

"Who says that I do?" replied Stella with a shrug. "It's easy to be objective about another person's challenges. Though, like I've said to you before, I've always known myself pretty well. I know that I'm a mixture of sweet and sour, nice and nasty – the whole spectrum. My mother was such a wild character when I was growing up in the 70's; she'd probably tried everything so she was never going to judge me for anything I got into. She might have found my being around inconvenient at times, but she always accepted me, just the way I was. 'She's her mother's daughter,' she used to say."

Stella leaned across the table and patted Lily's cheek. "The trouble with you is that you've been brought up to be such a polite, considerate girl that it feels wrong to you to be selfish and put your needs first."

"It doesn't sound much like Oneness," grumbled Lily, still feeling out of sorts.

"But it is," replied Stella. "Ananda Giri says we are responsible for our personal growth first and foremost and, from there, we can be much more effective and balanced because we're coming from a place of resourcefulness instead of always trying to put out fires with a half-empty bucket."

Lily sighed, "When am I ever going to get all this?"

"It's not an exam, it's a journey," laughed Stella, "and the fun of a journey is that it opens our minds to new ways of thinking and being. Perfection would be pretty boring – which is just as well because I'm not likely to get there!"

She stood to her feet. "Ananda Giri*ji* is starting in ten minutes. I bet you'll get exactly what you need from the session to put things in perspective."

"I hope so," Lily smiled, her sense of humour returning. "Just don't make me sit next to Daphne!"

Chapter 17

Ananda Giri observed the room silently for some minutes before speaking. They were used to his delivery now and Scott had got over his desire to get the young Indian a cup of coffee to wake him up. The teacher had been surprised, during yesterday morning's question and answer session, when someone asked him why he paused for so long during the delivery of his lectures. Another pause had followed the question and then he had replied, as Rajesh had done earlier in the week, "I do not speak until The Divine gives me something to say."

Not a bad policy, Scott had thought, to wait until you had something valid to communicate, instead of just trotting out the same polished discourse, without considering whether it was actually relevant to the audience. There were a lot of public speakers, be they politicians or Board members, who would benefit from that wisdom. He was going to take a leaf out of Ananda Giri's book and consider what to say in future, instead of pre-empting a response or reacting to who had spoken previously. People had always expected him to be the comedian, the life and soul of an event, but it had left him feeling superficial at times. Taking a couple of seconds of consideration before speaking was powerful. His father had always been very deliberate in the way he communicated; it was part of the reason he was so well-respected.

He looked across the room and saw Lily sitting with Stella in the back right-hand corner of the hall. It was a good thing she wasn't in his immediate line of vision; it would have been a distraction and he wanted to concentrate on what Ananda Giri had to say. When they greeted each other this morning and she had been composed and friendly, their encounter last night didn't seem to have made her feel awkward towards him and he was glad. He was hopeful of finding the opportunity to speak to her properly before the end of the seminar and, if Gina's idea went according to plan, Thanksgiving was only a few weeks away.

"Yesterday I spoke to you about our need to be at ease with ourselves," began Ananda Giri. "When we reach this place of self-acceptance, we accept others as they are and conflict ceases. Though we can grasp this concept in theory, it has not been easy to achieve in practice, which is why grace has come to us in the gift of the blessing. The blessing results in the expansion of consciousness and is the phenomenon behind the message of Oneness. When the energy is transferred, either by the touch or the intention of the giver, it initiates a neuro-biological change in the brain." He paused once more, allowing the group to absorb this revolutionary information. "There are sixteen centres in the brain which are responsible for definitive experiences, such as sensory perception, the emotions of jealousy, hatred, love, fear, compassion, our sense of separation and connectedness and our ability to be creative and to learn," continued the young man. "The blessing results in the activation of certain centres and the de-activation of others. When we find ourselves in a situation which we interpret as being stressful or dangerous, chemicals will be fired off in the parietal lobes, which induces our response for fight or flight. This is an ancient survival response and is over-developed for our current way of life. A job interview is not attack from wild animals or danger from marauding tribes but, because of the chemicals released in our brain, it often elicits the same extreme response from us."

"He obviously hasn't had to go up before the hospital's Board of Governors," Tom whispered to Scott under his breath.

"That's his whole point," replied Scott, keeping his voice as low as possible. "We act as though these things are a matter of life and death, when they're not."

"This neuro-biochemical change allows the brain to respond calmly, bringing a shift in our perception and experience of life," continued Ananda Giri. "It is what allows us to see people as they are, instead of reacting to them as though they are our enemies. We see that our suffering comes not from the incident but from the way we have perceived it, imagining slight and offence where there is none. This re-balancing allows us to embrace every facet of our personalities, instead of being afraid of our anger, our laziness, our judgement. We accept ourselves as we truly are and become able to observe life, instead of seeing it through distorting filters. We can experience anything fully from this place, without fear, and it becomes joyous to us."

Ananda Giri continued to expound the benefits of the blessing, explaining that the effects deepened as a person received the energy transfer regularly. This made sense to Scott. Not only had he sensed the effect of the blessing going deeper each time he had experienced it but he could relate it to a fitness training or eating well; the effects were greater the longer you applied the principles.

There were other positive benefits. A personexperiencing the blessing regularly would become more relaxed and centred; the challenges of life wouldn't cease but they would feel less reactive to situations. Consequently, their health would improve as they would be firing off less debilitating chemicals into their nervous systems. One of the positive effects of reducing the constant release of neuro-peptides was greater clarity of thought, allowing people to be much more effective in their daily lives.

Scott glanced at Tom, who was listening to Ananda Giriattentively. He wouldpick his friend's brains after this morning's session and get a medical point of view.

"When we are calm, we are more receptive," the young teacher was saying. "We are open to the opportunities that come to us, instead of constantly struggling and striving to fulfil our desires. As we begin to experience our connectedness with the whole of the universe, we understand that we are part of the symphony of life. Our lives are a journey, being revealed a step at a time in the grand design; this journey begins with an understanding of where we are, not an obsession of where we want to be. The universe constantly evolves and expands; everything in life is an expression of the miraculous unfolding of The Divine."

Ananda Giri paused, looking calmly around the room. "Please close your eyes for a few moments and consider what you have heard this morning. The guides will be sending you an intent blessing so that these truths will become real to you, allowing you to experience the full effects of the blessing." The young men had joined him on stage and were silently observing the room. It struck Scott how congruently they worked together; it was far less about them producing a well-polished seminar and far more about them being in total accord with one another. A tangible example of Oneness, he thought, closing his eyes.

The familiar sensation of the blessing filled the room: calm, peace, bliss. Scott exhaled deeply, relaxing into the moment, soaking up the atmosphere. The blessing wouldn't be an easy phenomenon to explain back home. He had understood the teaching he had received and, although the concepts were new, they resonated with him. It made sense that the conflict in the world arose from a sense of being separate individuals; if we could see ourselves as being inter-related, each action being committed affecting the rest of humanity, of creation, then we would be far more careful about what we thought, how we lived. But the blessing was far more experiential than that; he would love for his family and his close friends to be able to have the same experience. He must ask Rajesh if any more seminars were going to be held over the next few months.

"Shanti, shanti, shanti." Ananda Giri's voice brought the period of contemplation and blessing to a close. Gradually, people in the room began to open their eyes. "You will be meeting with your guides this afternoon at three o'clock to continue the teaching. Thank you." Once again, he placed his palms together at chest height, in the traditional gesture of respect and, rising from his chair, left the hall accompanied by the guides.

"Wow! That was deep this morning," said Scott, turning to his friend.

"Yes," agreed Tom. "Their teaching is so profound."

"And what do you think about their claim that the blessing actually causes a neuro-biological change?"

"There is a lot of research going on at the moment at some of the major universities – Princeton's one, I think – studying the effects of conscious intention. It started out with studies on telepathy, back in the 60's but it's much more extensive now," said Tom. "Technology has advanced so much that science is able to monitor the activity of the brain and how it responds to the supposed transfer of energy, the effects of meditation, and so on – you know, there is some evidence that meditating on a regular basis actually prevents the brain from deteriorating. Fascinating."

"And could they prove that the blessing actually produces the effects Ananda Giri was talking about, like being less stressed or having greater powers of concentration?"

"Well, the statistics certainly indicate that these phenomena do have an effect; whether they would attribute it to a higher consciousness or put it down to being a placebo effect is debatable."

"But things are changing, Honey," said Gina, joining in the debate. "There has been so much research on the effects our thoughts and intentions have on a situation, or even on the material world. Look at the work Masaru Emoto has done with his work on water. It's hard to refute."

"I haven't heard of him," said Scott. "Who is he?"

"He's the Japanese guy that wrote The Hidden Messages in Water after extensive experimentation with water crystals," explained Tom.

"It's amazing," continued Gina enthusiastically. "He created a controlled environment where he studied the effect words or thoughts had on water. In some instances, the water was subjected to positive influences, a phrase like 'I love you' or 'thank you' would be taped to the water's container and others – negative words like 'I hate you' or ' I want to kill you' – would be taped on to others."

"What happened?" asked Scott, his curiosity aroused.

"When they froze the water that had been shown positive words, the crystals formed beautiful, complex patterns but on the water that had been shown negative words, the crystals that formed were deformed or, in some cases, couldn't form at all,"said Gina. "It's so clear that there is an underlying intelligence present in everything and admonishes us that we need to be aware of the effects our thoughts can have on other people. Think about it. The human body is around 70% water."

"That's kind of scary. Obviously, I know my actions affect other people but I'd never considered that my thoughts might have an effect, too," said Scott, shaking his head. "This is a whole new realm of thinking for me."

"Yes, it's new for all of us," agreed Gina, "but like I said, more and more evidence is coming in to back up this new standpoint. Before, it was only a small section of society, the yogis and hippies, that subscribed to these views but now, with the world in so much turmoil, more and more people are starting to sense that there needs to be a massive change for things to get better."

"It's a sobering thought," said Scott, solemnly.

"I actually think it's a really hopeful time," smiled Gina, reaching for her husband's hand. "Tom will tell you that when we started a family and had Luke, the world suddenly became a very scary place to me. I saw dangers everywhere that I had never considered before. I was sick with worry that we had brought a baby into such a turbulent world. The more bad news I saw in the media, the worse I felt."

"I was really worried about her," added Tom. "It was as though she was overwhelmed by all the cares of the world, like she felt them as if they were her own."

Gina nodded. "It was just like that. I kept saying to myself, over and over again, 'things have got to change, things have got to change'. It became like a mantra for me. And then it struck me: I was right, things had to change. I made the decision then that I would try to be part of the answer, instead of putting all my energy into focusing on how bad things were. Straight away, I was much calmer, it was as though, just by setting my intention, a weight had been lifted off me." She reflected for a moment before continuing.

"After that, all kinds of coincidences started happening: someone would give me an inspiring book or invite me to a talk and the underlying message was always the same: things needed to change in our world and it would come about gradually, as we decided to make a difference ourselves." Her expression was calm and certain as she continued. "And I've been aware of grace running through my life ever since. Being here this week has made me so certain that we're reaching a tipping point; mankind is going to evolve to another level, to really know the experience of Oneness that Ananda Giri has been talking about."

"I hope so," said Scott. "We certainly need it. You know, I'd really love it if I could effectively share what we've learned this week with my family. It would be so hard to explain. It would be great if they could experience the blessing."

"Geeze, Scott! Where have you been this week?" asked Tom, an incredulous grin spreading across his face. "That's the whole point of the seminar: tomorrow evening we're going to be initiated as blessing-givers."

Chapter 18

Lily and Stella arrived at the group meeting a little before three o'clock and were met by a flurry of excited chatter. Clearly, Scott hadn't been the only one who hadn't realised the implications of attending the seminar.

"Did you know about this, Stella? Tom and Gina seem to think we're going to become blessing-givers ourselves tomorrow." Daphne's tone, far from being pleased, indicated that she was piqued.

"Yes, I did know," replied Stella. "It was mentioned in the information pack that UPG sent out. Maybe you didn't fully understand that they were referring to a process called 'the blessing' rather than a general benediction, as it was out of context."

"Well, I'm sure it must have been worded very badly," replied Daphne huffily, going to sit down.

"What's upset her this time?" Lily whispered, as she and Stella settled into their seats.

"I expect she felt that she should have been the first to know, instead of one of the last," her friend replied in an undertone. "Poor old Daphne, so caught up in things that don't matter."

"Hey, ladies," said Scott, coming over to greet them. "That was quite a session with Ananda Giri this morning, wasn't it?"

"It was powerful stuff," agreed Lily, "and now we find out that we're going to be able to give the blessing, too. It's wonderful, I can't quite believe it."

"I know," said Scott. "It's awesome. Funny, I was wondering how I would be able to share the experience with my family and then Tom told me we were going to be initiated as blessing-givers tomorrow night."

"I wonder how it will happen," mused Lily.

"Rajesh will be able to tell us," said Stella. "Here he comes now."

"Good afternoon," said the guide, as he moved towards the front of the room and took his seat. "How are you all this afternoon?"

"Great, Rajesh," answered Brenda. "I'm so happy that we're going to be able to give the blessing to other people."

"What is the initiation process?" asked Scott. "What do we need to expect?"

"There is nothing to be concerned about," replied the guide, sensing his apprehension. "You will receive the blessing from the Oneness Beings, as usual, but their intent will be that, as you receive it, the power to be a blessing-giver will be transferred."

"But how will we know whether we've got it or not?" demanded Rod, gruffly. Lily exchanged a look of surprise with Stella who whispered, "Just goes to show, if you're in this atmosphere long enough, it'll get you in the end."

"You will know," Rajesh was addressing Rod's concerns. "When you give the blessing to others, they will experience the same effects as you have felt this week. As you give the blessing regularly, you will become more attuned to the energy flowing through you and feel its effects more strongly."

"What will that result in?" asked Tom, pushing his glasses back on to the bridge of his nose, a look of intense concentration on his face.

"Your sense of Oneness will increase," answered the guide. "Each time you give the blessing, you experience its power also. Your sense of intuition will increase because you will be more in tune with consciousness. From this place, you will be able to respond to situations and people more appropriately; as your own consciousness expands, you will have a sense of being in the flow of life," he smiled. "This is not to say that there will be an end to problems but, as your awareness increases, you will be able to receive the lesson in the experience and grow, instead of being overwhelmed with anxiety, struggling against circumstance. The challenges in life are what cause us to evolve, if we are open to the message they bring."

"It all sounds a bit idealistic," Rod was back on the defensive.

"But we need some kind of ideal to work towards," countered Gina. "Don't you think that's better than believing the world is going to hell in a handcart?" Rod grunted but he didn't contradict her.

"It's kind of hard to grasp, sometimes, this ethereal stuff," said Marcie. "I'm a very practical person; I like tangibility, material evidence. It's all new to me, trusting that a greater consciousness is running the show ... and yet ... there have been odd moments, all through my life, when I felt that there was some bigger influence. Moments of serendipity, strange coincidences."

"We all have those moments," said Rajesh. "We are all part of the same consciousness and, even at those times in our life when we have no knowledge or interest in this truth, our infinite self will grasp the opportunity to gain our attention, reminding us of our true nature."

"And this awareness of inter-connectedness is no longer the sole domain of spiritual groups," he continued. "Quantum physicists have shown that everything in the universe is made up of energy and that it is all inter-related. What happens on one side of the galaxy influences what happens on the other. No one thing is a separate event. Studying the way molecules behave has provided evidence that there is an intelligence behind the way the universe operates. Electrons behaves differently when they are observed, indicating that they have awareness, that they are not just mechanical components."

"Fancy you knowing about quantum physics in India," said Rod in admiration.

Smiling, the guide replied without any trace of irony, "We have the Internet, I am on Facebook."

As the group spilled out into the afternoon sunshine, waves of laughter spilled from Lily.

"That was so funny!" she said, dissolving into a fit of giggles. "I couldn't believe he was so ignorant about India. And the guides are obviously educated men. Does he think they live in little mud huts back at home?"

"Probably," grinned Stella. "Don't forget, the world probably begins and ends in Texas for Rod."

"Oh, I know, I know! I was just so amazed that he would come out with a remark like that."

"But it didn't annoy you, like before," observed her friend.

"No, I suppose it didn't," mused Lily. "I guess I've realised that's just the way he is; he's just clueless. Rajesh wasn't offended, so why should I be?"

"You've just illustrated Ananda Giri's point."

"Have I?" said Lily in surprise. "That's impressive."

"Yes," continued Stella. "The best gift you can give a person is to allow him to be himself."

"Well, it's nice to know all their hard work is paying off," smiled Lily, linking her arm through Stella's.

"What do you feel like doing now?" asked Stella, as they meandered back towards their bure. "Gina mentioned she might drop by for a cup of tea; we've got a couple of hours before the blessing this evening."

"I'd really like to go for a dip," said Lily. "It's been so muggy today, I thought I'd go down to the beach and find somewhere for a swim."

"Yes, it is stormy," agreed Stella. "A dip sounds like a good idea. I'd come along with you if I hadn't said I'd see Gina."

"Couldn't she come, too?"

"She's not keen on swimming at the moment," replied Stella. "Remember what she said on the boat?"

"Oh, yes. I'd forgotten," grinned Lily, "too much buoyancy."

"It's probably a little too hot for her to be waddling about at the moment anyway, poor love. Let me see." her brow furrowed in thought. "The beach on the far side of the port would be the best place to swim from. It has fewer pebbles to walk across than some of the others and it's not too far. You'd be able to swim and fit in a shower before the meeting." Reaching their temporary home, they mounted the steps to the porch and Stella made to settle herself in the swinging chair.

"That would be great. I'll put my swimsuit on under my shorts and head down there straight away." Lily trotted off to retrieve her costume from her case, threw her clothes on again and, grabbing her beach bag, headed out.

"See you later. Say hi to Gina for me."

It didn't take her long to reach the beach, which, she was glad to see, was deserted. Kicking off her flip-flops she sunk her toes into the moist sand which was cool and inviting. She wriggled out of her clothes and dropped them into her bag, anticipating the pleasure of the water's refreshing caress as she stepped into the ocean.

It was colder than she had expected. Lily stood with the water lapping around her knees, deciding whether she would go in further. She was a bit of a wimp about swimming in cold water. She laughed as the scene triggered a childhood memory.

They'd been on holiday down in Cornwall and their parents had taken them to the beach for the day. It had been a typical English summer, with more rain than sunshine. The little seaside town didn't have much entertainment to offer on wet days, all its activities being focused on the beach. Lily and her brother had grown restless and petulant from being confined indoors too long and were driving their mother crazy. As soon as the first glimpse of sunshine appeared after being absent for three days, she had whisked them down to the beach to run about and blow off some steam.

They'd charged about, whooping and hollering, chasing the seagulls that had launched themselves briefly into the air, only to alight again a few feet out of reach. Lily had quickly become disdainful of the game, calling it boring, and had wandered off to explore the rock pools that were formed under the cliffs that overhung the sandy expanse, protecting it from exposure.

It was not long before Paul had come looking for her, pestering her to swim with him.

"It's too cold," she had replied. "Mummy says it needs the sun on it for a couple of days, for it to warm up."

"No, no! It's warm," he had assured her. "I've just been in, look. We could practise our diving from that rock."

Lily had looked at her brother suspiciously but had seen that his trunks were wet. Paul hated swimming in the cold even more than she did, so she knew he must have been telling the truth.

"OK," she had said bossily. "I'll give you your next diving lesson, then. You watch me and I'll show you how it's done."

She should have realised that something was wrong when Paul didn't reply with his usual whiney "Why do you always have to be first?" She had taken up her position at the edge of the rock, hands together above her head, and belly-flopped into the sea. The water was so cold it had taken her breath away. She surfaced, her teeth chattering, her eyes as big as saucers.

"You t-told me it was w-warm!" she had stammered to Paul as he knelt above her on the rock, his expression gleeful.

"I got you good, didn't I?" he had gloated. "I sat down in a rock pool so it looked like I'd been in the sea."

"You wait till I get hold of you! You'll be sorry!" she had threatened, starting to splash for the beach.

"Catch me if you can!" he had sung as he had raced away to

hide.

She had been so furious, she remembered. She'd hunted for him all afternoon without success. Eventually, when the sun was starting to drop in the sky, her parents had grown concerned and joined in the search. They'd eventually found him, curled up on a pile of old nets at the back of one of the fishermen's huts; she had found the door ajar and crept in. Paul was fast asleep, the picture of serenity, his blond hair curling against his cheek.

They were so relieved to find him they couldn't be cross, not even Lily. As their father lifted his son's somnolent form, Paul opened one sleepy eye and caught sight of his sister.

"You've got to admit, Lily, I got you! Your face was a picture!"

"Just you wait! I'll get you back," she had retorted but had reached out and squeezed his chubby calf affectionately as her father carried him past her.

She must give him a call when she got home; they'd both got caught up in their own lives and hadn't seen each other for a while. She'd like to remedy that, to spend more time with him and his family again.

What was it that had become their victory cry for the rest of the week, as they'd plunged in and out of the waves, defying the cold? That was it! Lily summoned up the courage of her younger self and shouting, 'Geronimo!' plunged beneath the water.

Chapter 19

"So where's Lily?" asked Gina, slowly climbing the steps to the porch. "I wanted a word with her."

"She's gone for a dip; she shouldn't be long. What was it you wanted to talk to her about?" asked Stella, inquisitively.

"Make me a cup of tea and I'll tell you," replied Gina. "It's a long story and I'm going to need some lubrication."

"Ooo, errr, Matron!" quipped Stella as she went to boil the kettle.

"So, tell me what's going on then." The two friends were sharing a pot of Earl Grey, enjoying its aromatic flavour.

"The other night, Scott finally realised he has feelings for Lily," began Gina.

"I know," said Stella with satisfaction. "She said he almost kissed her."

Gina raised her eyebrows. "He didn't tell me that, but he did say he's very serious about getting to know her better. He wanted us to help him find a way of spending time with her that wouldn't hurt Marcie, so I suggested we invite them up for Thanksgiving."

"Excellent idea!" enthused Stella. "Can I come?"

"No, you can't," said Gina, firmly. "You know you couldn't resist teasing them."

"I can be very discreet!" said Stella, huffily.

"I know you can be," replied her friend patiently, "but we both know how the urge to be mischievous overwhelms you. Besides, it's Thanksgiving. You're going to want to be with the boys."

"I suppose you're right," conceded Stella, "but you must let me know how things turn out."

"I'm sure they'll tell you themselves," said Gina. "I've got a feeling that those two will make a go of it."

"Well, it could be a bit tricky with them being on two continents but, from what Lily's told me, a lot of her work is Internet-based. As long as she's got access to a computer, she can pretty much work as normal."

"And you know how determined Scott can be when he's got the bit between his teeth," agreed Gina. "New York's only about a seven-hour flight from the UK anyway. Stranger things have happened."

"I hope it works out," sighed Stella. "I've grown very fond of Lily this week. She deserves to have a great man like Scott in her life."

"Stell! You've gone all romantic on me!" teased Gina.

"I have my romantic side," retorted Stella indignantly. "I just hope Lily will be co-operative. She was saying the other night that she's not prepared to sacrifice what she wants for her life just because a man comes along."

"Well, good for her," replied Gina. "That's exactly as it should be. I'm not worried, though. There's such a sense of purpose here this week, I'm sure all will be well."

Stella took a sip of her tea, watching the darkening horizon.

"I hope Lily gets back soon. Those clouds are coming in thick and fast. We're definitely in for a storm." As if to illustrate her point, thunder rumbled ominously in the distance. Stella stood up, her expression worried. "I'm going to go and find Nelson and ask him to drive down to the beach and pick Lily up. I don't like the look of this at all."

"No," agreed Gina. "The air has become really thick in the last few minutes. I hope it's not going to be like that storm we had here last summer."

The women exchanged anxious looks and, without further ado, Stella hurried down the steps to go in search of Nelson.

Lily hadn't swum for long. She had splashed about for a while then floated on her back, looking at the passing clouds, before she realised she was drifting quite a way down the beach. The current was stronger than she had expected and it made her nervous. She decided to make her way back on to the beach and then head back to the *bure* to have a leisurely shower before the meeting. It had taken quite a lot of effort to regain the shore and, reaching it, Lily felt quite worn out. She made her way slowly back to her beach bag, feeling the effects of both the fatigue and the anxiety she had just experienced. Glancing up, she saw that the clouds had deepened to an angry slate-grey and she knew she would be very lucky to get back to the *bure* before the storm broke. Sitting on the sand, she shrugged on her T-shirt and felt the first plump drops of rain. She pulled on her shorts hastily, slid her sandy feet into her flip-flops and hurried up the beach.

The rain began to fall heavily, soaking her completely; her hair fell in tendrils around her face and her clothes clung to her like a second skin. She felt as though she was a mermaid who had ventured on to *terra firma*.

A clap of thunder rumbled directly overhead, causing Lily to increase her pace. She must get under cover as soon as possible; the storm was beginning in earnest. Suddenly, a flash of forked lightning cracked through the air like gun-shot, hitting the ground about twenty feet to her left. Lily screamed in fright and started to run; she had never known such a violent storm and she was caught right in the middle of it.

Don't panic, she told herself, trying to calm her breathing and remember what buildings she had passed on her way to the beach. The driving rain distorted her sense of distance but she thought she remembered seeing a small health suite, which should be a little further up on the right. Another clap of thunder sounded overhead, making her ears ring and her chest contract as the adrenalin coursed through her body. You're nearly there, she kept saying to herself. Hold it together, Lily, you can do this.

A little way ahead, she saw a figure dart out from underneath the palm trees that lined the path and then stop suddenly, as though uncertain of what to do. Shielding her eyes, Lily peered through the rain to try and make out who had been caught in this terrible storm with her.

The figure's head was darting from side to side in panic. Lily recognised Daphne's bedraggled features and realised that the woman was terrified.

"Daphne!" she screamed, as loud as she could, aware that her voice was likely to be drowned amidst the clamour of the storm. "Daphne," she shouted again as she reached her, "we have to get inside, it's too dangerous to stay out here."

Daphne looked her blankly. "But we have to get to the meeting. It's starting in a few minutes."

Lily realised the older woman was too scared to make sense of what was going on and took hold of her arm.

"We'll go in a minute, when the rain has died off a bit," she said, leading her towards the small building ahead.

"Oh, yes. That's a good idea," Daphne conceded meekly, allowing Lily to steer her towards the health suite.

Thunder rent the air overhead once more, accompanied by another dramatic display of lightning. Daphne froze on the spot, gazing at Lily, her eyes wide with terror.

"I hate storms," she whimpered.

"We'll be inside in a minute, Daphne," said Lily firmly. "We have to keep moving."

Daphne didn't appear to have heard what had been said, but responded when Lily placed her hand on her back, walking her purposefully towards the building.

Reaching the health suite, Lily tried the door which, mercifully, was open. She pushed Daphne gently in ahead of her and was turning on the lights when she heard a deafening bang, as though a bomb had just gone off. Feeling disorientated, she couldn't relate to the second noise that had followed the explosion. What was it? Oh, yes! It sounded like something was falling.

A second crash reverberated around them, accompanied by a loud tearing sound. Lily whipped around to see what was happening but, as debris began to fall around them, the lights went out, throwing them into darkness.

Stella threw off the blanket that was serving as a makeshift raincoat and pushed open the door to the hall. Scanning its occupants anxiously, she spotted Tom and Gina and hurried over to them.

"Lily isn't here?"

"No!" replied Gina. "I thought you were going to ask Nelson to go and look for her."

"He'd already gone into the village on an errand," Stella answered. "I started to look for her myself but then the electric storm started and it was too dangerous. I hoped she'd come straight here."

"My God!" said Tom, his brow wrinkling in concern. "It's really hazardous out there. We were going to stay at our *bure* but we reasoned it would be better if we were all in the same place in case the power went down. What is Lily doing out in this?"

"She'd gone for a swim, near the port," replied Stella. "The storm came in so quickly, she must have been on her way back when the lightning started. She must have found somewhere to shelter."

"What's between the port and here, where she could have found cover?" asked Tom urgently.

"There's the diving shop, on the opposite side of the port," Stella racked her brain for anywhere else that Lily could have sought refuge, "and there's the health suite, part-way along the path to the reception building."

"Good. So there are some places she could have sheltered in," said Tom. "I hate to think of her outside in that weather."

"I'm frightened for her," said Gina in a small voice. "I've never seen lightning like that in my life. It struck the palm tree just in front of our *bure* and broke it in two. It was like something out of the Apocalypse."

"Hey, guys! What's up? You all look very worried." Scott and Marcie had come over to find out what was going on.

"Lily's missing," said Stella. "She would have been on her way back from the beach when the storm broke."

"You mean she's out in this?" Scott's expression was horrified.

"Lily's a sensible woman, Scott," Tom reassured his friend. "Stella says there are a couple of places where she could have found cover."

"But what if she's injured?" said Marcie, anxiously. "This storm might not blow out for hours; we can't just leave her out there and hope she'll be all right."

"I agree," said Scott. "I'm going to go and look for her."

"Now hang on a minute," said Tom, firmly. "We need to have some sort of a strategy before we go off, all gung-ho. Is there anyone else missing and how can we protect ourselves when we go out there?"

"Good thinking, Honey! I'll go and see if there is anyone else who hasn't made it to the hall." Gina started to check if anyone else was missing, glad to have something useful to occupy her.

"I think Nelson's jeep is fitted with a lightning rod; he requisitioned it from a light aircraft that crashed here fifteen years ago," Stella said to Tom. "I'll go and check if he's back."

"I'll come with you," said Scott.

The battered old jeep was parked in its usual spot, next to the reception. They could see that the rain had let up slightly and although the thunder was still rumbling, the clouds had moved out to sea and the lightning's frenzied war-dance now shot spears of light into the ocean.

"I'll check with Gina if anyone else is missing, grab Nelson and tell him we'll set off as soon as I get there."

"Right!" Stella pulled the blanket over her head again and dashed across to the reception.

Scott found Gina inside, talking to the guide Raksith.

"Daphne's missing, too," she said, as he approached.

"No-one else? Good. Stella's at reception, briefing Nelson. Tell Tom to go and get his emergency medical bag and bring it back here in case anyone's injured. We're setting off now."

"I will come with you," said the guide, his expression concerned.

"Great," said Scott. "Perhaps you'll provide us with some insurance against that angry lightning god."

"Maybe," replied Raksith, his lips twitching into a slight smile as they left the hall.

Chapter 20

"What happened?"

"I don't know," Lily replied. "It sounded like one of the palm trees came down on the porch. Are you OK?"

"Yes, I think so. Just shaken," replied Daphne, her voice trembling slightly.

"Me too! That lightning was spectacular. I've never felt such raw energy," said Lily, trying to peer out through the window.

"Don't remind me," said Daphne, shuddering. "Can you see anything?"

"Not really," replied Lily. "There's something blocking the door, it won't open, but I can't quite see what it is."

"This is a sort of gym, isn't it? Do you think they have any towels here that we could use to dry off?"

"Good idea! They probably have some candles, too. Let's have a look about and see what we can find," said Lily. "Take care you don't trip over those ceiling tiles that came down."

Between them they found a stack of towels underneath the reception desk and a number of large, cathedral-style candles.

"Looks like losing the power is a regular event," commented Lily. "Let's hope they've left us some matches. Ah! Here they are!" She lit a candle and the two women surveyed the room.

"Phew. We were lucky," said Lily, looking at the fallen debris. "It looks like whatever fell just missed the main structure. A little further over and the whole roof might have collapsed."

Daphne flopped down on to one of the pieces of weight-lifting equipment and put her head in her hands.

"Oh dear. I feel a little faint."

"That's quite understandable," Lily sympathised. "You've had a horrible shock – we both have." She handed Daphne one of the towels. "Dry yourself off and I'll see if I can find anything for us to change into."

She started to look through the cupboards in the reception area.

A few minutes later she emerged, giggling, from behind the counter, brandishing garishly-coloured tracksuits.

"Welcome to Pele," Lily read, pointing to the logo emblazoned across the front of the material. "Which colour would you like? Cerise-pink or turquoise-blue?"

"Dear me! I'm going to look like my aunt Gloria who retired to Orlando," said Daphne, looking perturbed. "Oh well. It's not the time to worry about that!" She extended her hand with a wry smile. "Turquoise, please."

Dressed in her very unstylish new pink attire, Lily took a candle over to the entrance and stared out again.

"It's jammed tight," she said, straining her weight against the door. "It looks like a telephone pole has come down out there."

"Be careful," Daphne warned her. "There's a crack in the glass, at the top. We don't want it to shatter and cut you to pieces."

"No, you're right," agreed Lily, gazing at the crack that zig-zagged across the top of the glass door, reminiscent of the lightning that had rent the sky earlier. "I'll check and see if there is a rear entrance."

She came back clutching a couple of snack bars and two cans of sports drink.

"There's only a small kitchen back there, but I found these. I guess there's nothing to do until someone comes to rescue us."

Daphne accepted half of the food and they sat munching in silence for the next few minutes.

"It's been a strange week, hasn't it?" said Lily, thinking back over the last few days. "I've had at least five life-changing events since I got here and now I can add Near-Death Experience to the list."

Daphne looked at her quietly for a few minutes before replying.

"Really? I haven't had any."

Lily was a little confused. "Haven't had any what?" she asked.

"Life-changing events," she replied. "I haven't had any."

"But surely you must have," argued Lily. "You're streets ahead of most of us with this stuff. I would have thought you'd be transported to seventh heaven, experiencing the blessing every day."

"Yes," said Daphne sadly, "so did I. But I've just been feeling left out in the cold."

"What do you mean?" Lily asked.

"Well, I understand the teaching that Ananda Giri and the guides have been giving us but I only seem to get it on an intellectual level." Daphne sighed in frustration. "Most of you have no idea what a privilege it is to receive such wisdom from these men, yet you've all been changed this week, even Rod."

Lily considered what the other woman was saying. "I know that I've changed this week. I feel much happier being me, just as I am." she said. "But I thought everyone was feeling like that."

"That's what I mean," replied Daphne impatiently. "Everyone is getting it but me. I've been having such a horrible time. I feel like the jealous brother in the story of the prodigal son and I hate myself."

"The prodigal son?"

Daphne darted a disbelieving look at the younger woman but explained without any further comment.

"It's from the Bible. A father has two sons. The younger one decides he wants his half of the father's fortune and the father gives it to him. He then goes off travelling and squanders the lot, coming home a few years later, penniless, cap in hand. The father, far from being angry, welcomes him with open arms and orders that a feast be prepared in celebration of his son's return. The older brother, who has worked diligently for his father all his life, is outraged and refuses to come to the feast. The father comes to his son and asks him why he is so angry, reminding him that all his riches have been available to the elder son at any time. 'My son was lost,' he tells him, 'and now he is found; of course I'm going to celebrate his return.'"

"And you feel like the older brother?" Lily asked tentatively.

"Yes, I do," answered Daphne, her expression distressed. "You guys joke around all the time, behaving inappropriately, talking about sex, and it's as though grace has been handed to you on a plate. It just seems so unfair," she finished, jutting her chin defiantly.

"Well, I do understand what you mean," said Lily. "My brother could be as naughty as he liked, growing up, but my mum rarely even told him off. It used to make me furious."

Daphne seemed slightly mollified. "It just doesn't seem fair, when I've dedicated my life to helping people and searching out the truth."

"Maybe that's it," said Lily carefully, not wanting to lose the rapport she seemed to have developed with the older woman. "You know so much more about philosophy and spirituality than most of us. Perhaps you've got more to unlearn. Ananda Giri said that we feel that we are separate because of our conditioning; maybe you had preconceived ideas about this week that you need to let go of, so that you can enjoy the experience."

Daphne was looking a little defensive again but she didn't contradict the younger woman.

"And look at your life," Lily continued. "You've just said that you've dedicated yourself to trying to help people. You've probably neglected to look after your own interests better. I think you need to give yourself permission to go to the feast."

The older woman looked at Lily, an expression of wonder spreading across her face.

"Thank you, Lily! I think you're right! I've had an epiphany!"

Her expression changed, showing concern. "Oh! An epiphany is …"

"That's all right, Daphne," Lily interrupted her cheerfully. "I know what an epiphany is and even if I didn't, I could tell from the look on your face just now."

Daphne brightened again. "Sorry, dear, I didn't mean to be patronising. It's an unfortunate habit of mine. I really don't know why you've been so kind to me, when I've been such a bitch this week."

"Let's just say that the Brits are at their best in situations like this," smiled Lily. "It brings out our fighting spirit. We want to make Winston Churchill proud."

"Winston Churchill? But isn't he dead?" asked Daphne, looking confused.

"Never mind," laughed Lily, giving Daphne a hug. "Is there anything left in your can? Good! I want to propose a toast."

The two women raised their cans in the air and Lily solemnly proposed the toast:

"To the new liberated Daphne!"

"Hear, hear!" echoed Daphne, beaming. "Let's drink to the new me!"

Scott set off in the jeep with Nelson and Raksith. The storm had died down a little but driving rain still hammered against the windshield, making it difficult to see.

"Go easy, Nelson," Scott cautioned the old man. "There are a lot of fallen branches on the road."

"I'll go careful, Mr Scott, don't you worry. No point in us having an accident, too."

Scott's mouth turned down in a grimace at the old man's words. "I hope they haven't had an accident, either. Where do you think we should start looking first?"

"If we just follow the road to the port, we will pass all the places they might have found shelter," replied Nelson. "It's not far. We should find them in no time."

True to his word, Nelson proceeded carefully, steering the jeep expertly around the debris that the storm had strewn across the ground.

The thunder rumbled angrily again in the distance.

"Storm's moving away," commented Nelson, keeping his eyes on the road. "The worst is over now."

"I'm glad to hear it," said Scott, grimly. "I don't think I can remember seeing one as fierce as that before."

"No; worst storm since the hurricane here in 1969, I reckon," said Nelson. "There'll be a lot of clearing-up to do."

"It was indeed a magnificent storm," the guide said thoughtfully. "What is that building ahead on the left?"

"The gym."

"I believe we will find our friends inside," stated Raksith.

Giving the guide a quizzical look, Scott instructed the old man to pull up outside the health suite. As they approached, they saw a telephone pole had fallen sideways, crushing the porch and obstructing the entrance to the small building.

Colour draining from his face, Scott leapt out of the jeep and surveyed the damage.

"Lily!" he shouted. "Daphne! Are you in there?"

A few seconds later, Lily's face appeared on the other side of the glass, illuminated by the candle.

"We're both here," she called. "We're fine."

"Hang on," he replied, the relief flooding his body. "We're going to get you out of there."

"That pole's too big to move without a tractor," said Nelson, having taken stock of the situation. "We could get them out if we smash the lower door panel."

Scott shouted the plan to the women, instructing them to get as far away from the door as they could to avoid the flying glass. The pane gave way easily, casting fragments of glass into the air like tiny icicles.

"Be careful. Wrap your feet in whatever you can find," ordered Scott, "and be careful not to touch the frame on your way through."

"You go first, Daphne," said Lily. "I'll help you."

The older woman clambered nervously through the devastated door-frame with Lily holding on to her hand to help her balance. As soon as she was through, Nelson guided her to the jeep and installed her there safely, with a cup of tea from the flask they had brought with them.

"Come on, Lily, your turn." Scott extended his hand through the gap.

She grasped it firmly, steadying herself to negotiate the obstacle. Once outside, he helped her scramble over the pole that had demolished the front of the building.

Lily gave a low whistle as she looked at the wreckage. "That was close. We'd only just got inside when the pole came down. We could have been killed."

"Thank God you weren't," said Scott fervently. "I was so worried about you."

"Well, God's had more to do with it than you know," said Lily conspiratorially. "While we were trapped in there, Daphne had an epiphany."

"Is that like a colonic?" enquired Scott, his joke hiding the emotion that was threatening to overwhelm him.

"Are you never serious?" laughed Lily. "Here I am, survivor of a near-death experience and all you can think of is potty humour!"

"Come on," he chivvied her. "Let's get you into the jeep. I'm sure you'll feel better as soon as you're out of that charming outfit."

"I think it's rather fetching," replied Lily, scrambling into the back seat. "I'm going to have 'I survived Pele' embroidered on the back. Hello, Nelson! Hello, Raksith! Thank you for coming to rescue us."

"You're welcome, Miss Lily," grinned Nelson. "I never could resist a damsel in distress."

"What do you want to do, ladies?" asked Scott. "Joking apart, you've both had a very unpleasant experience. Do you want us to take you to your bures?"

"I'm feeling fine," replied Daphne. "I'd really like to catch the end of the blessing meeting. I've got so much to be thankful for after this evening."

"Me too," agreed Lily. "I want to be with all our friends."

Nelson dropped them outside and then headed over to the reception to see if any reports of the damage had come in.

Walking up the steps to the hall, Scott caught Lily's arm.

"Could I have a quick word?" he asked, his voice low.

"Yes, of course. Tell Stella we're just coming, would you, Daphne? I don't want her to worry. What is it Scott?" she asked anxiously. "You look a bit strange."

He waited until the door swung shut behind Daphne and Raksith before pulling Lily into his arms and kissing her hard on the mouth.

"I thought something might have happened to you," he mumbled into her hair, holding her tightly. "I was so worried."

"Scott," she whispered, reaching up to touch his face. "I'm fine. Everything's fine."

"I know, but I don't want to lose you, Lily," his expression was intense. "I want you in my life. Say you'll see me again after this week."

She gazed up at him, her face wreathed in smiles. "Yes, I'd like that."

He kissed her again, more gently and they stood holding each other, oblivious of time. Eventually, Lily unfurled herself from him.

"We'd better go in. They'll be worried about us."

"I know," he smiled, "come on then."

Opening the door, they crept into the hall.

"See you later," whispered Lily, going to join Stella and Daphne who had made a space for her. She sat down and was enfolded in a warm hug.

"I'm so glad you're safe," said Stella, gratefully.

"Of course I am," replied Lily. "How could anything really bad happen in this enchanted atmosphere?"

"Well, I can see Daphne's had a transformation and that would definitely have taken an enchantment. What happened?"

"I'll let her tell you herself," Lily whispered. "I don't want to steal her thunder."

Stella wrinkled her nose. "I don't know if that metaphor is apt or in poor taste, given the circumstances."

Lily squeezed her friend's hand affectionately and turned her attention to the Oneness Beings, who were giving the blessing. She was glad to see that the meeting had proceeded as normal. There was nothing anyone else could do except wait after the rescue party had been organised; she wouldn't have wanted anyone to substitute this wonderful experience with hours of useless worry. She had a sense that everything had unfolded just as it should have. A piece of divine theatre had been played out that afternoon, containing all the elements of a good play: drama, humour, courage, reconciliation and love.

"Lily," Rajesh gestured to her, "It's your turn to go up."

Smiling, she walked towards the front of the hall, her heart full of gratitude.

Chapter 21

The Ultimate Peer Group was assembled in the hall to hear Ananda Giri's final lecture. Lily couldn't believe the final day had arrived so quickly. When she looked back at the woman who had arrived on the island so full of insecurities and doubts, she felt as thoughshe'd been transformed; a caterpillar turning into a butterfly, as in her vision. This week had far surpassed all her expectations; she felt very happy and grateful to have received such grace.

Scott caught her eye from across the room. They had spoken briefly after the blessing last night and had agreed that although it would be hard, they would keep their contact to a minimum for their final hours on the island. They both felt sure there would be plenty of time for them to be together in the near future. She smiled at him and then turned her attention to the young teacher seated in his white chair.

"Good morning," Ananda Giri's melodic voice filled the room. "I am very happy to see you all here this morning. We are very grateful that nobody has been injured, despite the ferocity of last evening's storm. However, the villagers have suffered some damage to their property; we have offered to go and help them in any way that we can after the meeting this morning. Those of you who wish to join us would be most welcome." A murmur of assent rippled around the room.

"Thank you," he said, noting the response. "Nelson will be organising the work teams, please speak to him when you leave."

"This is a most auspicious day," he continued. "Tonight, when you receive the blessing from the Oneness Beings, you will become blessing-givers yourselves. When you return home, you will be able to share this profound gift with those you love. The blessing can be transferred either by contact, in the manner you have experienced this week, or by the power of your intention when you ask The Divine to touch an individual or a group of people, as you have experienced this week."

"I know that some of you are concerned at the thought of how you will explain this phenomenon. Trust that grace will bring the right people into your path and, when it does, that you will be given the right words to say, to meet them where they are. Many people will not be able to grasp the concept initially, but they will be drawn to you when they see your ease with yourselves and your willingness to accept them just as they are," he smiled. "If you consider the reservations some of you felt only a few days ago, you will see that the grace is more powerful than the intellect."

"He's not wrong, there," whispered Daphne, who was sitting next to Lily. "Once I let go of all my rationalising and just opened up, I really felt the blessing last night."

Lily squeezed her hand, relishing the older woman's happiness. Daphne was transformed; her pompous demeanour was gone and she was really enjoying herself. She had discarded her usual austere navy trouser-suit and was wearing a pretty floral dress.

Another butterfly, thought Lily to herself. It's so good to see people set free.

"We are well aware that we are living in challenging times," continued Ananda Giri, his tone serious. "Despite what you see, remember that you are making a positive difference in the world. Through the teachings you have received and the experience of the blessing, your consciousness has expanded this week; this will have a positive effect on the collective consciousness of mankind. In the same way that a small lamp can dispel much darkness, your presence will start to dispel the fear and sense of separation in those around you. They will see your happiness, peace and inner harmony and will begin to realise that the hopelessness they feel is an illusion; it is only real if they perceive it to be." He paused and a hush settled over the room as the group weighed up his words.

"The journey you have begun here this week will continue after you leave. Your guides wish to remain in contact with you, so that they may continue to give you their support and hear about your experiences. We encourage you to meet with each other as often as possible, so that you may each give the blessing to each other and those you come into contact with who wish to share the experience. These small beginnings will cause a ripple effect, gradually influencing not only your friends and families but your colleagues, your communities, your cities and your countries."

"You have heard about the hundredth monkey principle?" Ananda Giri scanned the room and, seeing there was a mixed response, he continued. "I will explain. Some years ago, scientists were studying a tribe of monkeys on a remote Japanese island. They had introduced sweet potatoes on to the island to see how the study group would respond to this new food source. The monkeys discovered the sweet potatoes, dug them up and attempted to eat them but they could not work out how to clean off the soil. The soil made the vegetable unpleasant to eat so the monkeys discarded them."

"Eventually, some of the younger monkeys discovered that if they washed the sweet potatoes in the ocean, they were good to eat. The rest of the tribe observed this for a while, then gradually more and more of the monkeys followed the example of the young ones until all but a few of the tribe were eating the potatoes."

"As this occurred, it was discovered that in other study groups, in remote locations that had no contact with the first group, other monkeys were learning to wash and eat sweet potatoes simultaneously. It appeared that as the first group of monkeys expanded their learning and understanding, it affected the collective consciousness of the rest of the species."

He smiled. "We believe that this will happen with the human race; it will only take a small percentage of awakened people to tip the consciousness of the whole, bringing us to the next stage of our evolution."

Resting his hands in his lap, the teacher observed the room quietly once more before continuing.

"Do any of you have any questions you would like to ask this morning?"

John raised his hand at the front of the room and Ananda Giri gestured for him to speak.

"Ananda Giri," he began. "First of all, I would like to thank you and the guides for the wonderful gift you have given us this week. My wife and I are so grateful that we were able to share this experience." He glanced lovingly at Brenda, who was nodding enthusiastically. "I would like to ask your advice about how we can share the blessing with our community," John continued. "We come from a Christian background and are worried that people might think we've become caught up with a cult."

"Thank you for your question," the young man replied. "The message of Oneness is not a new religion or a cult, but rather a gift from The Divine to enhance your own beliefs. If you follow Christ, Buddha or Mohammed, we say continue to follow them; we do not wish anyone to give up their faith. The blessing will enhance their experience of The Divine in whichever way it is manifested to them. If you do not follow any of the traditional religions and feel closest to God in nature, then, through the blessing, you will have a greater appreciation of this expression of God."

"The blessing is an experiential phenomenon; as a person feels its effects, he will be less concerned with doctrine. As he has a very real, very personal experience of The Divine, he will not need to look to anyone else to define his reality."

A tall, blond-haired man from Raksith's group was the next person to ask Ananda Giri a question. "I have a twin brother who is an alcoholic. Can the blessing help him?"

"Yes, of course," replied the teacher. "When someone has developed such an addiction, he will need much understanding and support to become free of it; you will have to show him that he is greatly loved, just as he is now. This will help him to be free of the guilt and self-loathing that prevents him reaching out to you. The blessing will help both to address the emotional pain and suffering that has caused him to become an alcoholic and to heal his body." He opened his hands. "You must be patient; at first he may not even be willing to experience the phenomenon but you can send him the blessing by the power of the intention and ask your friends here to do the same. Gradually, as you continue to ask for grace to flow, he will begin to desire to be well and respond to the help offered him."

The next person to raise her hand was an elegant woman in her late forties that Lily recognised from the reception evening. "My ex-husband left me with a six-week-old baby when I was only nineteen. I've never been able to get over it. Can the blessing help me let go of my bitterness towards him?"

Ananda Giri sat in silence for a moment before answering.

"As you receive the blessing, you can ask The Divine to help you to let go of the anger and pain that you have carried for so many years. When you allow yourself to feel your suffering fully, the charges will dissolve and you will be free of the pain. It may not happen all at once, as it has been part of your identity for many years; it would be too traumatic for you to face all of the pain at once. As you gradually become free of it, you will be able to forgive him and, in doing so, grace will be able to flow into his life also. It is important to remember this: as we open our hearts in search of healing, it flows through us to those around us, releasing them from their suffering, too."

The questions continued for a few more minutes before Ananda Giri called a halt. "Now we must go and help the villagers and share in their suffering, so that they can share in our joy." He stood and, placing his hands together at his chest, inclined his head slightly.

"Namaste."

"I can't quite believe this has been our final session with him," said Lily wistfully, watching him leave the hall with the guides.

"I know," sighed Stella. "It's been an auspicious occasion, as the guides would say. But you can always go to one of the courses at the Oneness University in India."

"They run courses?"

"Yes, that's how UPG heard about them. One of their directors had apparently been on a course himself and decided it had to be made available to the members; he clearly made the right decision."

"No doubt," replied Lily. "I feel like this week has just whetted my appetite, I want to experience more."

"Me too!" Stella's eyes twinkled. "That's why I've offered them the resort on a regular basis."

"Darn! I wish I had a resort of my own to tempt them with," teased Lily.

"Don't be silly! You're part of the furniture now," retorted Stella. "You're welcome to come here any time you want to. In fact, I insist that we look at our diaries before we leave. What are you doing for Christmas?"

"Thank you!" Lily flung her arms around her friend. "You're so generous!"

"I am, aren't I?" she grinned, "You are deeply in my debt."

Chapter 22

The old school bus was at the gates of the resort, waiting to take the next group down to the village. One busload had already been dropped off and had been assigned the task of clearing any fallen branches that were obstructing the roads. This group was going to help repair the damage caused to the school buildings and Nelson, realising that he had a great opportunity to take advantage of so much willing labour, had coerced them into painting the classrooms, too.

"It'll be fun," said Tom. "With so many of us working together, we'll get it done in no time."

"Yes," agreed Stella, "I don't think the school has had much attention since the last big storm. It will be good to give it a bit of a face-lift."

Raksith and Rajesh had combined their two groups for the task; when everyone was assembled, they clambered on board and Nelson drove the short distance through the luscious rain forest to the school.

They passed some villagers on the road who smiled and waved, calling out their usual friendly greeting, "Welcome, welcome."

It reminded Lily of her journey from the airport the day they had arrived on the island. She'd had no idea of what would unfold for her in those few short days and marvelled, once again, at everything she had experienced on Pele.

"Who would have thought one week could change your life so radically?" she remarked to Stella, who was sitting beside her at the back of the bus.

"Who, indeed?" replied her friend. "I'm still bowled over by the change in Daphne," she continued, watching the older woman chatting and laughing with one of Raksith's group. "Such a transformation. I know The Divine specialises in miracles but I'm particularly impressed with that one."

"I know, it's great, isn't it?" grinned Lily. "Poor Daphne was so terrified, she actually let down her guard. I think that's what made the difference; it meant she had a real experience of grace instead of seeing it as a concept."

"We've each had our own special moments this week, haven't we?" mused Stella. "John and Brenda still look as though they're on their honeymoon."

"And it's lovely the way he keeps looking at her so proudly," said Lily. "He doesn't seem threatened by her new-found confidence at all."

"No," agreed Stella. "He told me over dinner last night that they're both remembering to be the people they were when they first got married, before they accepted all the labels society pins on you: husband, wife, mother, father, realtor, church organist, pillar of the community," she smiled. "They've decided to drop the masks and just get back to being who they are: John and Brenda."

"Back to basics," said Lily, watching Brenda smooth John's hair off his forehead.

Stella nodded. "Deepak Chopra says that one of the characteristics of the universe is pure simplicity. We're so much more at ease when we keep things simple."

"And what about you?" asked Lily. "What's been the most significant thing that's happened to you this week?"

"Me?" Stella thought for a moment. "I've loved every moment of being here, listening to Ananda Giri, meeting you, spending time with Gina and Tom. I suppose the most important thing I've understood is that, although I'd stopped grieving for Robert, I wasn't open to letting another man come into my life; I didn't think I could stand the pain again." Her eyes sparkled as she continued. "I've let that fear go this week and I know the right man will come along now. There are so many wonderful things in life to enjoy. I need someone to share them with."

"I know what you mean," agreed Lily, watching Scott talking

to Tom at the front of the bus. As though he felt her eyes on him, Scott turned and smiled.

"I'm so glad the two of you have talked," said Stella.

"Yes," smiled Lily, a blush colouring her cheeks. "I was particularly glad of that bit of divine intervention. There I was, bravely renouncing my feelings for him and, voilà, the obstacles were removed."

"More like, crraaackk!" laughed Stella, miming a lightning bolt, as they pulled up outside the school.

"But I want to help!" wailed Gina, trying to carry an armful of paintbrushes.

"You were only allowed to come on the condition that you sat down and did nothing," said Tom firmly, relieving her of her burden. "You can't clear branches and you can't paint; the smell will make you nauseous. Go and sit in the shade with your book."

"Not fair! There must be something I can do," said his wife truculently, plonking herself down in the shade of a hibiscus tree.

"I knew I shouldn't have let her come," sighed Tom. "I should have guessed all that compliant 'yes, Honey, I'll just come and read my book' was too good to be true."

"You knew what you were getting into when you married the fiery little redhead," countered Stella, staggering past with two large tins of paint. "You've made your bed, so lie in it."

The women started on the painting, leaving the men to clear the heavy branches that were strewn around. Thankfully, there hadn't been too much structural damage. A young palm tree had fallen across the clearing that served as a rugby pitch and lay there like a fallen giant. A local man had provided his tractor and Nelson's enthusiastic recruits were already chaining the tree to it and working out how they could tow it away, with minimal damage to the pitch.

"One, two, three, heave!" shouted Rod, as the men used their combined strength to lift the trunk enough for the chains to pass underneath. He was in his element, like a Major General commanding his troops.

Not such a loner any more, thought Lily as she carried more paint over to the classrooms.

The biggest tragedy was that one of the store-houses had been burnt down when a bolt of lightning had set fire to its roof, incinerating the meagre supply of sports equipment owned by the school. The boys were wildly enthusiastic about rugby and cricket and were devastated by their loss.

The headmaster had come out to greet them when they arrived, to offer his thanks and explain what needed to be done. As soon as Scott heard about the sports equipment, he pledged that Pioneer Sports would supply the school with whatever they needed.

"We are already so grateful for your support," responded the headmaster, looking overwhelmed. "We are a small community and it would have taken us weeks to repair the damage done by the storm. That you offer us such a generous gift … I do not know how to thank you."

"There is really no need," replied Scott modestly. "Just give me a list of what you need and we'll get it shipped to you."

"What wonderful colours," enthused Lily, looking at the aqua-blue, lilac and pale-yellow paints they'd been given. "I wish my classroom had been painted in one of these cheerful shades when I was at school."

"Mmm," agreed Stella. "I seem to remember my boarding school favoured a lot of beige. Probably one of the reasons I was so bored. No visual stimulation at all, unless the grammar school boys came over to use our tennis courts."

"I bet you were the bane of your teachers' lives," said Lily, rolling her eyes.

"Tried to be," her friend replied cheerfully.

Daphne came over to look at the paints. "Oohh! Let's nab that lovely blue," she said, seizing the tin. "Raksith's girls are going to start in here. Let's take this next door."

Stella grabbed the second tin, leaving Marcie, Brenda and Lily to bring a supply of brushes and turpentine. They set to work with enthusiasm, daubing the cheerful colour on the walls, quickly transforming the dreary classroom.

Lily was concentrating on the edges where the walls reached the skirting boards, producing a neat boundary that the girls could paint up to. Brenda and Marcie were up step-ladders, edging the ceiling, and Stella and Daphne, who had commandeered the large brushes, were applying paint to the walls in bold swathes.

"This is so much fun!" said Daphne. "I feel as though I'm back in my art lesson at college. It's a shame we don't have a radio to listen to." She began to hum part of a melody that Lily recognised as a Christina Aguilera hit.

"… I am beautiful, no matter what they say, words can't bring me down …"

"I am beautiful, in every single way," echoed Marcie, from the top of her step-ladder. *"So don't you bring me down today."*

Soon all five women were belting out the chorus, celebrating their femininity, their friendship and everything that they had shared over the last few days.

"Sing it again," demanded Gina, putting her head around the door. "I'm not missing out on this!"

Pausing from their tussle with the palm tree, the men heard the song drift across the clearing from the open window.

"Girl power!" said Tom, grinning at Scott. "You've got to love it."

"Wonderful creatures, women!" commented John. "I'm glad Brenda's found her girlishness again."

"And that Daphne's changed from an ugly duckling to a swan," added Rod appreciatively. "I must get her number before we leave."

A few hours later, tired but elated, the group gathered in the shade at the edge of the clearing to accept the refreshments that the staff had prepared for them. The children, who had been under strict instructions to concentrate on their lessons when the busloads of people had arrived, now offered their guests plates of the freshly-prepared fruit, with shy smiles and curious glances.

Rajesh produced a tennis ball from his pocket, causing a flurry of excitement. One of the older boys ran off back into his classroom, returning with a small branch that had been fashioned into a bat and soon an impromptu game of cricket was underway.

The guides proved to be excellent cricketers, consistently bowling out the Americans who couldn't quite grasp that the makeshift bat needed to be held facing downwards, instead of being swung at shoulder height.

"Out!" Raksith's call was heard again and again as Ananda Giri bowled them out. Eventually Stella couldn't stand it any longer.

"Come on Lily! You must have played cricket with your brother, growing up. Let's show these boys how it's done."

"No, no," protested Lily. "I was always scared of that nasty hard ball. I'm rubbish. I bet you can show them, though."

"Captain of the girls' under-eighteen cricket team; took us to the national finals," affirmed Stella, walking towards the game.

Ananda Giri smiled at her as she came in to bat. "Ready?"

"Oh, yes! Bring it on!"

The ball flew in a graceful arc. Stella had anticipated his bowl perfectly; she hit the ball with a resounding thwack, sending it way across the clearing. The schoolboys whooped with delight and chased after it, speeding across the grass. It was recovered quickly but not before Stella had scored sixty-three runs. Her winning streak continued for the next twenty minutes, before Ananda Giri changed his strategy and she was bowled out.

"Well done, Stella!" the cries rang out as she walked off the pitch.

"Thank you, thank you!" responded Stella, pretending to bob a curtsey to her fans.

Gina eased herself down on the grass next to Lily.

"Hey, Honey, I haven't had the chance to ask you yet; what are you doing over Thanksgiving?"

"Thanksgiving? That's at the end of November, isn't it?" asked Lily. "Nothing, as far as I know. Why?"

"Tom and I would like you to come and stay with us, meet all our tribe," smiled the redhead.

"I'd love to!" exclaimed Lily. "I've got loads of leave due to me. I'll speak to my boss as soon as I get back."

"And," Gina's smile widened, "Scott's going to be joining us, too."

"Oh! Gina! You're an angel!" Lily kissed her on both cheeks in delight.

"My pleasure," she replied. "I love happy endings, I'm glad to help a little with this one."

Lily shook her head in amazement. "I had no idea I would make such wonderful friends this week."

"It's been an extraordinary week, hasn't it?" said Gina, surveying the group. The game of cricket was still in full swing; Daphne and Marcie were trying to learn the steps of a native dance from some of the young girls and the rest of the group were sitting around chatting or relaxing peacefully in the warmth of the afternoon. She had the feeling of being in complete accord with everyone there.

"More so than we know," she murmured to herself. "Life will never be the same again."

Chapter 23

There was a great sense of anticipation as the group filtered into the main *bure* for the final time. When they left here this evening they would be blessing-givers, able to share the grace that they had experienced during their time there.

Looking around the room, Lily noticed that the women were wearing vibrant colours, as though the flowering of their hearts was reflected in their clothes. She smoothed her jade dress and smiled; she remembered reading somewhere that green was the colour of the heart chakra.

The Oneness Beings were guided into the room and took up their places on the platform. She closed her eyes in meditation, savouring the peaceful atmosphere, feeling a sense of connection to everyone in the room. The *Moola Mantra* was playing in the background, as before. Lily knew that each time she heard that piece of music, she would be transported back to this time and place.

The guides began to call people forward; Lily watched them receive the blessing, celebrating with each one as they received their gift. She smiled as she saw Tom and Gina go forward together, followed by John and Brenda. Despite the significance of the evening, it proceeded as tranquilly as usual; from time to time a gale of laughter filled the room but the predominant feeling was one of bliss. She was flooded by a sense of awe that the universe had conspired to bring her to this place, at this moment. It was an amazing thought. As if reading her mind, Stella spoke.

"You know, most people hardly ever experience a feeling that comes anywhere close to this, unless it's a momentous occasion like childbirth. What a privilege to have been here."

Lily nodded. Words couldn't express adequately the gratitude she felt for this week, not only for herself but for everyone in the hall; it had been a truly precious time.

Stella went up to receive the blessing and Rajesh motioned to Lily to follow. Standing in front of them, Lily felt their joy; as this gift was bestowed through them, they knew that its effect would be far-reaching, touching people all over the world. She felt as though she was floating on a cloud of joy as she returned to her seat. She was a blessing- giver! She would be able to share this beautiful experience with her family and her friends.

People continued to go forward until everyone had experienced their initiation. The Oneness Beings were then led from the stage and the group waited quietly for the guides to explain how to proceed. Raksith addressed them from the front of the room.

"We would like you to form small groups and begin to give the blessing to each other, just as we have given it to you. Remember, it is a gift of grace that flows through you; you are the instrument, not the source. You do not need to worry about how it will happen, or what to do. Just place your hands gently on the person's head for as long as feels appropriate and then move on to the next person."

Lily and Stella joined Daphne, John and Brenda. Placing their chairs in a circle, they looked expectantly at one another, wondering how to start.

"Who wants to go first?" asked Stella.

"May I?" asked Brenda, shyly. "I've been so looking forward to this moment."

"Of course," Stella replied, as the rest of them nodded their agreement. "Go ahead."

Lily closed her eyes and waited for her turn to come, happy to be able to enjoy the deep sense of peace that pervaded the place. After a few moments, she felt Brenda's hands alight softly on her head; the blessing flowed into her, gently imbuing her with the same sense of bliss she had come to expect. The feeling increased when John and then Stella touched her head; each blessing seemed to cause it to deepen. Lily had the very unromantic analogy of drain cleaner come into her head and she smiled to herself. She was confident by now that The Divine had a sense of humour and was not offended by any thoughts or feelings that she might have. I'm loved and accepted, just as I am, she reminded herself and felt a rush of appreciation for this truth that had so liberated her.

Feeling another person standing over her, she opened her eyes briefly. Daphne's face held an expression of such serenity that she was unrecognisable as the woman who had arrived on Pele. The years seemed to have fallen away, softening the lines that had been etched by unhappiness and disappointment. Daphne had, at last, learned to be at ease with herself and the healing this had brought her was already evident. Sometimes the universe does have to shout to get our attention, Lily thought; I'll never look at a thunderstorm in the same way again.

Lily was the last person left in the group to give the blessing. As she stood to her feet, she felt deeply honoured to be able to return the gift to those who had given it to her. Placing her hands on their heads and allowing the blessing to pour through them, she felt a strong sense of love and connection to each of the group and to everyone else she had met that week: Ananda Giri, the guides, the Oneness Beings, Nelson and the villagers. As she passed around the group, more images flooded her mind: her parents, her brother and his family, Matt, Josh and Charlotte, as well as many people she hadn't even thought of for years. As their faces appeared, she sent them love and blessings, too, asking The Divine to touch their lives, just as her life had been touched. She smiled, watching their images pass before her eyes, knowing that the answer had already been given.

Lily returned to her seat, cherishing the final moments of the meeting. A few minutes later, everyone in the hall had undergone their first experience as a blessing-giver and Raksith spoke to them once again.

"We are very happy that you have become blessing-givers this evening. As you share this gift with others, they will come to a greater sense of ease with themselves, as you have done this week. This is the first step in the realisation that there can be an end to our sense of separation from each other and, from there, the experience of Oneness arises. The awakening that has begun in your lives this week will continue; we will continue to support you and ask that you support each other." He gestured to the other guides who were spread throughout the hall. "We will be available this evening; if you should have any questions you would like to ask us, please come and speak to us." He opened his hands. "The restaurant has prepared a special meal for you this evening. Now go and enjoy the food and each other's company, this is a time to celebrate. Namaste."

"Rajesh," Lily went to speak to the guide before she left the hall. "I just wanted to tell you how grateful I am for your teaching this week and particularly for the blessing you gave me in our private meeting."

"You are very welcome," replied Rajesh, modestly. "I like helping people; it has made me very happy to be here this week, to see grace touching your lives and causing your hearts to flower. I am sure that we will meet again at the auspicious moment."

"I trust that we will," smiled Lily, sensing that it wouldn't be too long before that meeting took place.

"I can't believe this is our last evening," said Daphne tearfully, as they began to walk towards the restaurant. "Just as I was learning to appreciate you all."

"Don't worry! We'll keep in touch," Lily reassured her, "and there'll be a UPG meeting again soon."

"It's not until January," Daphne replied mournfully. "That's months away."

"Well, we'll just have to get our heads together and sort out a reunion before then," said Stella. "Why don't you all try to come back here for Christmas? Lily's already coming."

"Stella! That's great!" cried Daphne. "I'd love to come! Count me in!"

"What's all the commotion?" asked Tom, as he and Gina caught up with the three women.

"I've decided it's 'open island' for Christmas," said Stella. "I'll expect you and the brood, of course."

"Great idea, Stell!" enthused Tom. "Are you sure you don't mind putting up with the six of us?"

"It'll be seven," interjected Gina, patting her stomach. "This little one will have made an appearance by then."

"The more the merrier," replied Stella firmly. "The resort is open anyway, so it's not as if I'll have to arrange to cook for you all. It's funny, we had a cancellation last week, from a Saudi sheik; he'd rented half the resort for his family but they decided they'd rather go to the Swiss Alps instead. Now I know why."

"I've always wanted to spend Christmas on a tropical island," sighed Lily happily. "Another dream coming true."

"Your wish is my command," smiled Stella.

The staff had decorated the restaurant as though it was already Christmas. Gold and silver streamers were draped tastefully from the ceiling and the tables were strewn with tiny coloured stars.

"It's so pretty," gasped Gina. "Like a fairy grotto."

"We thought we'd go for a magical atmosphere," said Stella, looking pleased, "to remind us of what a special week it's been."

They headed to their regular table, joining the rest of the group already seated there.

"Hey, guys!" John greeted them. "How was that for you?"

"It was lovely," said Gina, lowering herself into a chair. "Serene and peaceful. I could do that all day."

"Yes," agreed Tom, "though I was a bit disappointed it wasn't more dramatic. I thought I might feel waves of electricity passing through me."

"You've been watching too many sci-fi movies, Honey!" smiled Gina affectionately. "This isn't *The X-men*, you know."

Tom grinned sheepishly. "I've always wanted to be a super-hero."

"Hasn't every little boy?" said Scott, joining in the conversation. "I used to sleep in my Batman cape until I was eight."

"Eight!" retorted Marcie teasingly. "Your mother told me it was eighteen! She had to get rid of it when you went to college!"

"Are none of my secrets safe?" asked Scott, shaking his head sadly.

"I had quite an unusual sensation," said Brenda, steering the conversation back to John's question. "I felt the energy was pouring through my hands like gently-trickling water. Did anyone else feel something like that?"

"My hands felt all tingly when I was giving the blessing," said Rod, his fork poised in the air. "What?" he raised an eyebrow. "You all look surprised that the dunce of the class should get special effects. Rajesh did tell us it was a gift, you know, not something that we've earned."

Stella laughed. "Well said, Rod! We all need to remember it's a gift; we're only the instruments that grace flows through, not its source."

"Yes, I like what you just said about us being instruments, Stella," added Lily. "So the notes are always going to come out differently, even when the same melody is played."

"Very nicely put," said Daphne, patting her hand without any trace of patronisation. "Very poetic."

The group continued to laugh and joke over their meal, sharing the moments that had been special for them over the last few days. Stella took lots of photos, promising to send them all a CD of copies over the next few weeks. They exchanged addresses and contact numbers, knowing it wasn't just an empty gesture; they had become so close over their time together that they genuinely wanted to stay in touch.

"I feel as though I've known you all for years," said Brenda, smiling around the table. "I can't wait until we get together again at the next UPG event."

"That reminds me," said Stella, "I wanted to let the rest of you know that you're all invited back here for a Christmas reunion. We thought the January UPG event was too far away." A ripple of applause greeted Stella's announcement.

"Stell, you're the best!" said Scott. "Come on, people! Raise your glasses, I'd like to propose a toast: let's drink to Stella and Christmas on Fantasy Island."

Epilogue

"Stella!" shrieked Brenda, dropping her bags and rushing over to her friend. "You're looking amazing!" she added, enveloping her friend in a hug.

"It must be the glow of love," she replied. "Stephen, this is Brenda and here comes her lovely husband, John."

"It's a pleasure to meet you, Brenda," said Stephen, kissing her on both cheeks, causing her to blush.

"It's wonderful to meet you, too," she replied. "Stella's told us so much about you."

"Don't worry, none of the rude bits!" quipped Stella smiling at him.

"Oh, I'm sure you have, Stell," replied Stephen shrewdly. "Everyone knows you can't resist a good story."

She grinned. "I plead the fifth amendment."

"Stephen," John extended his hand in greeting. "Good to meet you, buddy. Looks like Stella's met her match at last."

"John! What are you trying to say?" exclaimed Stella, giving him a hug.

"That you're a handful!" he laughed, returning the embrace.

"Where are Lily and Scott?" asked Brenda.

"Up at the waterfall," Stella replied. "Whenever they visit, it's the first place they head to. They should be back soon. Let's get you settled into your *bure* so that you can relax and settle in." She walked ahead with Brenda; the two men followed, exchanging easy conversation and getting to know each other a little.

"Stephen seems like a great guy," said Brenda quietly. "I'm really thrilled for you both."

"He's delightful," agreed Stella happily, "and, as John pointed out so astutely, a good match for me. He doesn't stand any nonsense."

"Well, that's just as it should be," said Brenda affably. "You would have trampled all over him in your high heels otherwise.

How long have you been together now?"

"A little over nine months," Stella replied. "You know that Stephen owns the gallery that hosted my photography exhibition in New York last Easter? We got together not long after that."

"Yes, we were sorry to miss the exhibition. Lily told us how good it was," said Brenda. "How is she getting on living in New York, by the way?"

"She's kept her flat in London and she goes back every other month, especially since she's so much closer to her mother these days, but she's loving the Big Apple and I'm loving having her there," said Stella cheerfully. "She's still overseeing the teen online forum and her book has gone to the publishers this week for its final edit. Her feet have hardly touched the ground since she moved out in May."

"It's been the same for all of us since the Oneness seminar," said Brenda. "I can't believe so much has happened in less than eighteen months."

"It's been an amazing time," agreed Stella. "Is your Oneness group still going strong?"

"Oh, yes," enthused Brenda. "We've had to start holding meetings weekly, people were so hungry to receive the blessing. Some of them have invited us to come to their homes, so that their family members can have the experience. We've heard so many stories of rifts being healed, teenagers giving up the bad company they'd been keeping, marriages being saved. It's so great to see grace flowing in peoples' lives and the healing that it brings."

"I know. Since my mother went through the process, she's been very active in organising inspired speakers to come to New York. There are so many wonderful people out there, sharing the message that we need to raise our consciousness: Marianne Williamson, Ekhart Tolle, Dr John Demartini. The guests give their talks and then the blessing is offered to anyone who wants to receive it afterwards.

It's really united all the blessing groups in the city, given them a common focus. I'm really proud of her."

"That really is Oneness in action, isn't it?" said Brenda admiringly.

"She was always good at organising big social events," grinned Stella, "but I never thought she'd turn her hand to raising the collective consciousness. Just goes to show you; you never know what will happen when The Divine moves."

"Is your mother here yet? I'd love to meet her."

"The families arrive tomorrow, I wanted us to have a little private reunion today," replied Stella. "Just our extended group."

"So where is everyone else? Is Daphne here, yet?"

"Daphne flew in yesterday with Tom and Gina's clan; they're all out on the boat," said Stella, "and Rod's arriving this evening on the five o'clock flight."

"What about Marcie?" asked Brenda.

"She couldn't make it in the end, she was really disappointed," replied Stella. "Victor's brother is getting married this weekend, too, and he's the best man. There was no way they could get out of it; you know what those big Italian clans are like."

"What a shame! I was really looking forward to seeing them again," said Brenda.

"Come and do a little shopping in New York sometime," invited Stella. "You know any of us would love to have you – John, too, if you can persuade him to come along."

"I'd love to," smiled Brenda.

They reached the *bure* that Stella had chosen for them, located at the edge of the ocean with views across the bay.

"I always forget how beautiful it is," sighed Brenda, gratefully. "Thank you, Stella, for remembering."

"You're very welcome," smiled her host, "it's your home from home. Dinner is at seven o'clock, up at the main house. It's a bit early but we have to consider the children. We don't want them becoming fractious from lack of sleep."

"Seven it is," said Brenda, kissing her cheek. "We'll see you up there."

A little before 7:00 p.m. that evening, the friends gathered in Stella's beautiful open-plan salon to celebrate Scott and Lily's imminent marriage. The couple were a few minutes late and entered the room to a round of applause.

"Well done, Scott!" called Rod. "You've persuaded her to go through with it after all."

"Hey, man," said Scott, clapping the Texan on his shoulder. "It was a near thing, but begging seemed to do the trick."

"I didn't need any persuading," said Lily, kissing Rod on the cheek. "I'm very much looking forward to becoming Mrs Scott Randall on Friday."

The children had launched themselves on Scott and were squealing with delight.

"Will you play baseball with us tomorrow? Will you?" cried Jesse, the seven-year-old.

"You promised you would."

"Now, Honey, you must promise not to wear Scott out if he plays baseball with you," said Gina, disengaging her children from Scott's limbs. "He's getting married in two days."

"I'd love to play ball with the kids," said Scott, kissing Gina hello. "You're looking as radiant as ever, by the way. Where's Daisy?"

"She's over there, with Tom," she smiled. "She certainly is a daddy's girl, that one."

"Hey, Scott! Ready for the big day?" enquired Tom. "Excuse me for not getting up. My daughter's just decided to go to sleep."

"I'm more than ready," grinned Scott. "You got the rings, groom's man?"

"They're safely back at our bure," smiled Tom reassuringly.

"She's just like a little cherub," whispered Lily, bending over the sleeping baby. "She looks so serene."

"She's been like that since day one," confided Gina. "I wish we'd known about the blessing with the other four."

"Hey, fella! How did the fund-raiser go for the sports scholarship foundation?" Stephen asked Scott, shaking his hand enthusiastically. "I'm sorry I missed it; we had an important private view that evening."

"It was awesome!" replied Scott, his face lighting up. "We got three other big names in the industry to add their support. It's great that they want to pool resources, instead of the usual competitiveness. We think a couple of the runners that we're supporting might have a hope in the next Olympics. It's so rewarding to see those kids opening up, realising that they have another option besides drugs or getting involved in gangs."

"You've started an amazing project, Scott," said Stephen, admiringly. "You should be proud of yourself."

Daphne came over to Lily and enveloped her in an affectionate hug. "You look gorgeous," she said. "All sun-kissed and glowing. You're going to make a beautiful bride."

"And look at you!" said Lily, looking at her friend in delight. "I love your new haircut, it's so soft and feminine."

"Thank you," replied Daphne, evidently pleased. "I found a great new hairdresser."

"John, Brenda! It's good to see you, too," said Lily, going over to greet them. "We're so glad everybody's been able to make it," she said, looking appreciatively around the room. "We know it was a lot to ask, being so close to Christmas."

"Honey, we wouldn't have missed it for the world," replied

Brenda, taking her hands affectionately. "You and Scott are like family. Where else would we be?"

"Now I'm getting all tearful," said Lily, her voice quavering.

"No tears!" said Stella firmly. "We're here to celebrate. Let's go through to the dining room, shall we? They're almost ready to serve dinner."

Sitting at the large mahogany table, the friends were served the mouth-watering fare of the island: succulent fish lay on beds of exotic vegetables, accompanied by crisp salads and bowls of steaming rice.

"This is a real feast, Stella," said Scott, approvingly.

"Yes, thanks Stella," came the chorus from around the table.

"They're just preparing themselves for Friday," said Stella. "This is a pale shadow of what the chef has planned for the wedding."

"I'm going to make the most of this now," said Lily, tucking into her food with gusto. "I'll probably be too excited to eat much on Friday."

"Hey! Slow down," said Scott, laughing at his fiancée's enthusiasm. "If you carry on like that, you're not going to be able to get into your dress."

"What a thing to say to a bride-to-be!" tutted Daphne, shaking her head in mock disapproval. "So, are you two preserving tradition and not seeing each other tomorrow?"

"Absolutely not," said Scott. "This marriage is not going to start off by being influenced by superstition. We know we don't have to be afraid of any bad luck."

"No," smiled Gina, "it certainly wasn't luck that brought the two of you together."

"You're so right," said Scott softly, watching Lily across the table. "That was definitely grace."

"Grace has touched all of our lives so profoundly," said Tom. "Gina's customers expect a blessing with their pot of tea these days.

It's amazing how people are open to hearing about Oneness."

"People are searching for hope," said Gina. "They don't care how far-fetched the concept of the blessing is; once they've experienced its effects and felt that sense of calm and ease, they want more of it. I've never had so many customers! People come in because they sense the tea-rooms have a nice atmosphere and then pretty soon they're regular customers," she smiled. "They hear people talking about the blessing and it makes them curious. I never force it on anyone, so they just watch and listen and, in the end, when they're confident that they haven't stumbled across some kind of cult, they start asking questions, asking me to send blessings to their grandmother, things like that. Eventually, they usually ask for themselves," she sighed happily. "It's what I always wanted when I opened the tea-rooms: to provide a refuge for people, somewhere they could escape from the chaos for a little while. I had no idea where that dream would lead me."

"Who would have thought our lives would be so enriched as a result of that seminar?" added John thoughtfully.

Lily looked at her friends, remembering how different they'd all been when they first met, including herself: Brenda so shy; Daphne so pompous; Stella so tactless. Well, some things didn't change. She smiled to herself, recalling her vehement dislike of everyone on that first evening; thankfully, the truth she'd heard in the teaching that week had set her free. Learning to love and accept herself, just as she was, had allowed her to accept other people on the same terms. She would be eternally thankful for that shift in perception. Sitting here, with the man she loved and the people she considered to be her dearest friends in the world, Lily felt flooded by a wave of gratitude that swelled her heart.

"Thank you," was her silent prayer to The Divine. "Thank you for showing me how much I'm loved."

About the author

Felicity Lerouge studied English and Creative Writing at the University of North London.

She continued her education, taking a diploma in Freelance Writing with the London School of Journalism, passing with honours. Having gone through the Blessing process in Fiji in May, 2007 she was inspired to capture her experiences, resulting in Changing the Channel, Felicity's debut novel.

www.felicitylerouge.com

Lightning Source UK Ltd.
Milton Keynes UK

176114UK00001B/1/P

9 781905 823550